Killer Cocktail & Other Short Stories

Killer Cocktail

A Patricia Fisher Mystery Short Story

Steve Higgs

Table of Contents

More Books by Steve Higgs

Free Books and More

Party

'Remind me how you got invited to this party,' I asked as the limousine we were in swung into a gated residence and houses the size of small townships came into view between the trees on either side of the winding street. Staring out the window, the car passed a man out walking his dog and my eyes bugged out of my head. 'Barbie, I think that was Tom Cruise!' Beside me, Jermaine spun his head around so fast that I thought it might fly off his shoulders. His eyes had been scanning the road for celebrities since we left the dock an hour ago.

In a voice that almost sounded bored, my pretty gym instructor friend said, 'Celebrities are two a penny here, Patty. Besides, they have to live somewhere.'

My name is Patricia Fisher, I'm a middle-aged English lady currently separated from her husband of thirty years and staying in the biggest suite on board the world's finest cruise liner. How all that came about, especially the bit about my separation and my suite is a long story for another time. It's a good one though because just a few weeks ago I was cleaning houses for a living; now I have a butler!

My floating home, the Aurelia, had docked in Los Angeles two days ago. LA is Barbie's hometown, but I had been surprised when she asked me if I wanted to come to a party with her. I am fifty-three years old to Barbie's twenty-two and I am frumpy and a little plump where Barbie is a size zero goddess with flowing blonde hair and a Hollywood smile. Despite that, she and I had become good friends over the last few weeks and she thought I was the perfect person to take with her. Actually, what she said was, 'I can't invite any of the boys because they will think it is a date and most of the girls are off shopping.'

I secretly wondered if she had invited me because her gay BFF, Jermaine was desperate to do some celebrity spotting. He was my butler and wouldn't go anywhere unless he was accompanying me.

'To answer your question,' said Barbie. 'The party is for a girl I went to school with. You might have heard of her…' she left that hanging in the air for a moment before providing the name, 'Kristina Khymera?'

'Kristina!' exclaimed Jermaine, so startled that he dropped his perfect Downton Abbey butler's fake accent for a moment and spoke with his true Jamaican voice. 'We're going to Kristina Khymera's house for a party?' He had one hand on his chest and the other on the ceiling to steady himself. He looked like he might faint.

'Um… yes?' replied Barbie. 'Her personal assistant is another girl I went to school with. Kristina and Melanie were such devoted friends back then that I guess it was inevitable for them to end up working together.'

'Is she someone I should have heard of?' I asked, a little worried that I was showing my age and she was some famous popstar I had never come across but everyone under thirty would know by sight or sound.

Jermaine exchanged a glance with Barbie before he said, 'She's the queen of YouTube. She made like two-hundred million dollars last year.'

'Doing what?' I asked, my tone unavoidably incredulous.

'Well… nothing really,' replied Jermaine. 'I mean, she gives advice and tells people what she thinks about different things and she is so popular that everyone fights to advertise on her feed and that is how she makes money.'

'That and personal appearances,' added Barbie. 'She has a very full calendar and I hear Pepsi is talking about getting her on their Superbowl advert next year. Anyway, Melanie saw from my social update that I was in town, so she invited me and told me to bring whoever I wanted.'

The limousine took us through downtown Los Angeles from the port in Long Beach in just over an hour and had been climbing steadily uphill for the last ten minutes as it wound into the hills overlooking the urban sprawl below.

'Nearly there,' said Barbie, turning in her rear-facing seat to talk to the driver. He cruised along the street for another minute before turning right into a long driveway that ended abruptly at a set of wrought iron gates. He spoke into the speaker mounted at window height and as the gates swung open, he proceeded through them and into lush green gardens filled with so many trees the house wasn't visible.

Silently, my brain said, 'Wow.'

It was another minute before we came through the trees to find the house beyond. It filled the landscape in every direction except up. 'Now I know what two-hundred million buys,' I commented in awe.

Barbie said, 'Oh, this isn't hers. Her mother owns the house. That's where the real money is.'

'Who is her mother?' I had to know.

'Some old singer. Apparently, she had some hits in the seventies. Mary Lou Winstead, I think her stage name is.'

I laughed at Barbie's answer. 'Mary Blue Wilshaw?'

'Yeah, that might be it,' she shrugged.

Acknowledging that I was more than twice the age of the two people I was with, I supplied some history. 'Mary Blue Wilshaw was the biggest artist of her time. She was a hit machine, singing about free love at a time when the world couldn't get enough of it. She headlined at Woodstock. You must have heard of Woodstock?' Barbie shrugged in response. 'Well, I was a child when she was cracking out her records, but she had a long career. Seriously though, this is like saying you haven't heard of Elvis.' Barbie looked at Jermaine, but he also shrugged, too intent on staring out the window to comment but it was clear he hadn't heard of her either.

The car pulled to a stop in front of the house before I could say anything else and Jermaine bailed out of his side before the engine died, his excitement turning him from reserved, dignified butler, into dribbling starstruck fool. The chauffeur opened my door and advised he would be back for us at ten o'clock, but that we could call for him to collect us at any point.

As I was straightening my skirt, the front door flew open and a young woman exploded out of it. She had crazy blonde hair that looked like it had been styled by holding it in front of a jet engine, and blue-sparkly makeup that zig-zagged across her face. She yelled, 'Barbie!' and held her hands aloft as she screamed. In her right hand she held a selfie stick with a camera attached and was screaming at Barbie then talking to the camera, then talking to Barbie again like she was giving commentary.

Next to me, and in reaction to her friend, Barbie also screamed before she too held up her arms and ran at the other woman yelling, 'Kristina!'

They met at her doorway and hugged like old friends might. All the while, Kristina held the selfie stick in such a way that she was in shot. Then, another scream lit the air as a third woman joined the hug, her voice a high-pitched squeal as she too shouted, 'Barbie!'

'Melanie!' replied Barbie with an equally bonkers level of excitement, all the while being caught on film by Kristina who was trying to talk to the camera while they were having a three-way hug.

I really wanted to hold up my arms and scream and then shout, 'Patricia!' just to see what would happen, but I refrained, choosing instead to wait patiently with Jermaine until Barbie remembered us. At my side, Jermaine was positively vibrating with excitement.

Barbie took that moment to extract herself though. 'Gosh, I am forgetting my friends,' she said. 'This is Jermaine; he and I work on the cruise ship together.' She held out her right arm to indicate my butler. 'And this is...'

'Your mother,' supplied Kristina. 'How could I ever forget you, Mrs Berkeley. So wonderful to see you again.' Before I knew it, the girl with the crazy hair and makeup was hugging and air-kissing me.

'Um, no, I'm...' I tried to explain.

'Can't talk now, sorry, got other guests to entertain,' she said, cutting me off. 'Catch up properly later. Love you.' She blew a kiss and skipped back into the house yelling excitedly, 'Come on Melanie, I need you to remind me the names of all my friends you invited. Barbie, come on, I need you to meet people.'

Melanie grimaced slightly, whispering an apology for Kristina, but as she turned to go, Barbie called her back. 'Quickly, Melanie. Has Kristina got a boyfriend at the moment?'

'No,' laughed Melanie. 'No, don't worry, Barbie.' Then another shout, this time from inside the house, and she dashed after her employer/friend leaving us to let ourselves in.

'What was all that about?' I asked.

Barbie chuckled. 'Kristina had always had a thing for older men. Once or twice it caused embarrassing situations. None worse than the time Melanie and I called for her, got let in by her mum, and found her half naked with our sixty-two-year-old chemistry teacher.'

'Wowza,' said Jermaine.

'Just don't go mentioning it,' Barbie advised. Music was drifting out from the house in an enticing way. But we stared at each other, waiting for someone to say something until Barbie took the lead; she was the one familiar with the place after all.

Her usual breezy smile in place, she clapped her hands together, looped her arms through mine and Jermaine's and we all skipped into the giant house like Dorothy and friends on the yellow-brick road.

It all felt a little weird, but I had no idea someone was going to be dead ten minutes later.

The Ex-boyfriend

Inside the house it was just as palatial as one might expect. Polished marble floors, what looked like gold leaf painted onto the walls, and paintings that looked like and probably were original Monet's dotted here and there. Kristina had a lot of friends; there had to be more than one hundred people in the place, and that was just in the room that I could see. They weren't all young, but most of them were, the average age of the crowd somewhere below twenty-five. I told myself to suck it up, have a cocktail and enjoy myself even though I was old enough to be mum to most people in the room.

The front door opened onto a wide lobby area that looked down over what I took to be the living area. Beyond it I could see corridors and other rooms coming off from the large room and having seen the front aspect of the house, I knew there was a lot of it I wasn't currently seeing. Wide spiral stairs led down to the main living area where the crowd was congregated, and a powerful bass beat was pumping in from somewhere outside. The crowd of party guests inside were spilled out through a set of open folding doors onto a patio area that led to a pool and ornate gardens. People were dancing and smiling, and boys were chatting up girls and girls were chatting up boys and my two companions were far more excited to be here than I was. I fixed a smile on my face, determined that I wasn't going to let my discomfort spoil their fun.

I started forward but Jermaine's feet were planted firmly on the ground while his jaw hung open. 'That's Sirius Bizniz,' he said while pointed into the crowd below.

'Where?' asked Barbie, suddenly interested.

I said, 'Who?' having no idea if Sirius was even a person. It was an odd name if it was.

'Oh, my God, you're right,' Barbie squeaked. 'I love him!'

They were both staring into the crowd still as I stood forgotten to one side. Remembering me for a moment, but without taking his eyes off the crowd below, Jermaine hissed out the side of his mouth, 'He's a rap star. He had a massive hit last year with B**** Don't be Ovulating Tonight.'

'He called his song what?' I asked incredulously, then had to quell my natural desire to give the gentleman in question a stern talking to about women.

Now it was Barbie's turn to point. 'That looks like Bubba Taylor,' she said to Jermaine, then for my purposes, she added, 'He's a quarterback in the NFL.'

Then Jermaine grabbed Barbie's shoulder, gripping it hard enough that she squeaked her discomfort. 'What?' she demanded.

Jermaine's mouth flapped a couple of times as he tried to get the words out. 'I just spotted Charlize Mercury.'

'Oh, I've actually heard of her,' I said, feeling pleased with myself.

'Charlize is a guy,' whispered Barbie. 'Goodness, he's so pretty.'

They appeared to be gawping at a man in a dress. I gave up at that point; it was supposed to be a party and I didn't have a drink. To have any hope of enjoying myself, I required some lubrication.

Looking about, I spotted a bar along the right wall of the room. It was a permanent feature, not something set up for the party but the two men working there looked to be hired in. They wore black waistcoats with crisp white shirts and black bow ties. One was shaking up a cocktail, pulling all the moves as he flipped the silver shaker into the air, spun on the spot like

Michael Jackson and caught it one handed. The two girls waiting for him to pour their drinks looked about ready to swoon.

'Hey, babe,' I spun my head to see who had spoken, but of course the comment wasn't aimed at me. Barbie was the intended target though she had to look down at the man that had spoken. He had black hair with a ginger streak dyed through one side of it and sported a mustache that could be best described at fluff. In heels, Barbie was over six feet tall but the six inches he was giving away didn't seem to perturb him. 'Say hi to my audience, gorgeous?'

Barbie simply lifted an eyebrow.

'Yeah, I'm something of an internet star.' The man had a camera on the end of a selfie stick, just like Kristina. I didn't understand it, but kept my mouth shut out of fear I would sound like a dinosaur. Keeping her in frame, the man swung around so he was in the picture with Barbie right behind him, then he leaned backward to look up at her. He was trying to impress her and failing badly. 'Paul Rodriguez,' he said. 'But you probably already knew that.' He indicated to a handful of other boys who were standing nearby and also filming him. 'This is my entourage. But what I need for my show is some real sex appeal and babe you've got it. Maybe later you and I can talk about how I can make you famous.' He left that hanging in the air for a while, waiting for Barbie to express her excitement at the prospect. When she said nothing and glanced about for an exit, he gave up on the act and went for broke. 'Okay, babe. You're hot, I'm famous and rich. Why don't we skip the games and get nipple to nipple?'

'Ewww,' said Barbie, pulling that same face I would if I found a dead rat in my handbag. 'Go away, you nasty little worm.'

Jermaine stepped up at that point, his wide shoulders, superior height, and withering stare enough to put the boy off.

'And don't talk to ladies like that,' I called after him as he slouched away. Then, to my friends, I said, 'I need a drink. What can I get you?'

'Madam, I shall bring you a drink,' Jermaine began saying but he stopped talking when I rudely held my hand in front of his face.

'Are you wearing butler clothes?' I demanded. He looked a little startled at the question, but it had been a rhetorical one. 'Then you are not currently my butler, Jermaine,' I stated with a genuine smile. He was always doing so much for me, the least I could do was fetch him a drink so he could mingle with the celebrities and famous people abounding in the room below.

'Very good, madam,' he conceded. Then seeing my expression, he corrected himself, 'Sorry Patricia.'

'That's better,' I replied. 'It's bad enough that I look like everyone's grandmother. I don't need you referring to me as madam the whole time as well. Now what'll it be?' I asked for a second time.

Barbie and Jermaine both asked for white wine spritzers, barely a drink at all in my opinion but I was sure the barman would be able to provide. I was going to allow myself an industrial strength gin and tonic. I might even have two.

Then a scream ripped through the room and I spun around, shocked by the sound only to find that three boys were lifting a young woman up to dump her in the pool, and she was playfully screaming in protest.

'What can I get you?' A space at the bar had opened up and the barman there was speaking to the back of my head. Satisfied that the scream wasn't the sound of someone being murdered, I turned around again to face him. 'I'll take two white wine spritzers please and a large gin and tonic. Do you have a selection of gins?' I asked. His professional smile was accompanied by a conspiratorial wink as he stepped to one side, revealing a range of bottles behind him.

A warm feeling of excitement spread though me as I eyed them up. Maybe this was going to be a good party after all. I watched as he chipped ice from a block on the counter at the back of the bar, ice flakes going into all three drinks as he expertly crafted my Hendricks and slimline with an ornately arranged slice of cucumber.

I thanked him, told myself the G&T was too full to carry and took a healthy slug before I set off to find Barbie and Jermaine. The cold liquid hit my taste buds and flashed messages all over my mouth: It was just how I liked it.

My friends were outside in the sun where Barbie was properly introducing Jermaine to Kristina. Jermaine had a goofy look on his face I had never seen before. In my presence, he was always so reserved and emotionless, almost robotic in his motions, but in the presence of an internet sensation, he was starstruck. I handed them both their drinks just as a man roughly my age appeared. He had drinks for Kristina and Melanie. He was good looking and tanned with an athletic frame that suggested he had been very fit as a younger man.

'Thank you, daddy,' she replied, giving him a quick air-kiss and making sure it was caught on the camera.

I noticed that Melanie looked away when he approached, refusing to make eye contact with him quite deliberately. I didn't say anything of course, but my senses told me there was something amiss, like Kristina's father had hit on her friend at some point and now Melanie thought he was slime but didn't feel she could say anything. She took the drink though and mumbled a thank you. He slipped away again, going about his business and the moment passed without anyone else noticing.

Kristina certainly hadn't noticed, but then I got the impression she didn't see or hear much that wasn't directly to do with her. She held the glass high, then slugged back the cocktail in one hit, throwing her head back and upending the glass into her mouth. Then she shuddered and yelled, 'Woooooo!' as loud as she could, getting a roar of approval from everyone around. 'Melanie, I need another one of those, babe,' she said, clearly giving an instruction to her friend/assistant. It was an odd dynamic, but if Melanie objected, I saw no sign of it.

'I'll be right back,' she said, turning away. I tracked her path into the house and decided it was time to mingle. The birthday girl was a bit much for me and as I walked away, she was once again ignoring those around her to talk to the camera. Was she live streaming her life? Was that how it worked?

I drifted inside, mostly being ignored by everyone around me and wondered if I might find Kristina's famous mother here. She was a decade and some older than me but closer to my age than most of the people present.

I distracted myself by looking at the art as I sipped my gin, but then a kerfuffle behind me drew my attention.

'What are you doing here?' a woman's voice demanded. I couldn't see who the voice belonged to through the crowd, but it sounded like Melanie. The voice was coming from near the bar, but I could only hear the raised voice of the woman as if the man was keeping his voice low in the hope his responses wouldn't be heard. 'What do you mean you were invited?' she demanded. 'I controlled the guest list.'

The crowd shifted, allowing me to see the argument as people nearby tried to be somewhere else. One of the handsome barmen said, 'Is this man bothering you, miss?'

'Hey, stay out of it, man,' the unnamed man replied, his voice rising to a volume I could hear for the first time. 'Melanie is just being dramatic. Tell the man you are just being dramatic, Melanie.'

In response she threw the drink she still held in her hand over his face. 'We broke up a month ago, Michael, you creep,' she yelled. Then as she tried to dart away, he grabbed her arm, his superior strength holding her in place easily. He looked mad now, colourful liquid dripping from his hair and soaking the upper half of his polo shirt.

The barman vaulted the bar, but he didn't get to do anything as Kristina's father arrived at that moment. Barrelling into the younger man, he tackled him to the ground.

Michael was struggling against his attacker but wasn't fighting him. 'Hey man, what the hell?' he asked, his voice loud enough to be heard by everyone in the room. 'I thought...'

'Shut up, kid,' Kristina's dad shot back. 'Don't make a scene now. Keep quiet and let's discuss this outside.'

On the floor, Michael let his bunched muscles relax, going flaccid beneath the older man to show his compliance. Just then, two security guards burst through the crowd, each positioning themselves on either side of Michael with their left hands out toward him in a warning sign for him to stop what he was doing and their right hands on the butt of their holstered weapons. It was complete overkill as Michael was already on the floor and offering no threat to anyone.

Their actions caused gasps to ripple around the room, audible despite the pumping bass outside.

'Desist, sir,' one instructed.

'Um, I have desisted,' he said, sounding confused as if they expected him to find a new level of surrender even though he was already on his back on the marble tile with his hands in sight.

'What's going on?' asked Kristina, cruising into the room as the crowd parted before her, the selfie-stick still capturing everything.

'Stay out of it, Kristina,' Michael warned, getting up now despite the close proximity of the nervous guards. He looked aggressive again. 'It's your fault Melanie and I broke up.'

'Damn right it is. I told her you were a bum, Michael,' Kristina sneered, then for the audience the other side of the camera she said, 'Hey girls, don't date Michael Torrence. He's a bum that will cheat on you and he has a small wiener.'

'Why you utter...' he started to say, then stopped mid-sentence when the security guards grabbed him, one getting hold of a wrist which he expertly turned against the joint while the other kicked him in the back of his right knee. The guards followed him down, forcing him to submit while he yelled and swore bloody vengeance. They didn't have cuffs but kept his arms behind his back as they lifted him up and dragged him from the room. As the trio passed me, Michael was still whining that he was there by invitation.

Calm settled, but only for a second as suddenly another set of raised voices could be heard above the music. This time Kristina was the loudest and she was poking a man in the chest and not paying attention to her camera for the first time since I arrived.

As the crowd moved, I saw that the man was Paul Rodriguez, the horrible little imp that had been so forward with Barbie. He had a smile on his face and was in turn talking to his own selfie-stick mounted camera. 'As you can see, lovely audience, make-believe socialite, Kristina, is having an eventful party. I don't know about you, but, hey!' he yelled as Kristina ripped the stick from his hand and snapped it in two over her knee.

'Try recording now,' she sneered.

'So, the great Kristina Khymera is afraid. You want people to see every aspect of your life, but only through your filter.' Paul crossed his arms in front of his chest and stared at her, his challenge obvious as he was joined by several interested looking companions, each with their own cameras pointed at her. It looked staged; like the man and his friends were ambushing her.

Kristina turned away from them to look for someone but didn't attempt to move. Not finding who she was looking for she raised her voice to shout, 'Melanie, how did Paul Rodriguez get in here?'

'You said to invite everyone,' Melanie replied, pushing her way through the crowd.

Kristina's face betrayed her disappointment. 'Are you stupid, Melanie? Paul's a two-bit hack trying to undermine me so he can steal some of my limelight. Only an idiot would add him to the guest list. You were supposed to invite my friends, not my enemies.' Then Kristina stood on her tiptoes to see over the press of people. 'Where's my security? I need my security!'

Melanie's face was a thunderous cloud as she replied through gritted teeth, 'You don't have any friends.'

Kristina's head swung around. 'What did you say?'

'All you do is step on people, Kristina. You forgot all your friends the moment you started making your own money. I had to invite anyone I could find, just so there were people in the background while you recorded your party.'

Behind Kristina, Paul Rodriguez and his cohort were all filming, moving about to get a better view and clearly loving the live drama they were capturing.

Melanie and Kristina were still facing each other down when Kristina lifted her own camera, fixed her smile and began jabbering away to the screen as if nothing much had happened. 'The price of success and talent,' she said, beginning to walk away. 'Two things Paul Rodriguez doesn't have. Don't take my word for it though. Go and check him out at PaulG123 hashtag the real life. It will keep you entertained with how amateur it is for about five minutes. Then you can come back to me. Go ahead, try it,' she urged.

Some of Paul's friends were checking whatever it was they had to check. One said, 'Hey, it's working. Your numbers are going through the roof!'

In the interim, Kristina was still talking to however many viewers she still had. 'Now, folks, to show you how real my life is, watch this.' She turned the camera around and pointed it at Melanie. 'Melanie, you're fired!'

'What?' screeched Melanie. 'You can't find your shoes without me.'

'You'll be paid up to the end of the month, but you can go now,' Kristina insisted, then spun on a heel and flounced away through the crowd all the while still talking to her camera.

An embarrassed silence settled over the room even though the bass was still thumping outside. Melanie had her head in her hands and looked about to cry. No one was approaching her which kicked in some kind of motherly instinct to make my feet move. Barbie got there first though, pushing her way through the press of people gawping at the scene.

She wrapped Melanie into a hug and was speaking softly to her as I arrived. 'She'll get over it and apologise later,' Barbie said.

'I'm not sure I want her to,' replied Melanie, her face buried in Barbie's shoulder. 'She can be so horrible and hurtful.'

'You did push her, Melanie,' Barbie said softly. 'She might not have many friends, but it wasn't cool to call her on it in public.'

'And she didn't have to call me stupid in public,' Melanie shot back.

'She never means it, Melanie. She needs you,' I stayed quiet, wondering if there was something I should be doing to help. This party was already something of a bust and I was looking forward to getting back to the ship.

'I know she needs me,' Melanie managed. 'She doesn't deserve me though.'

I decided this was a private conversation and drifted away again, looking for Jermaine so I could have him arrange for the limousine to come back for me. I would insist that he remain here if he wanted to and the driver could take me to see some of the tourist attractions I hadn't yet seen. As I walked away, I heard Melanie agree to get a fresh drink for Kristina and take it to her as a peace offering.

I spotted Jermaine on the other side of the room, his height making him easy to spot. He was chatting with a handsome man who had crewcut hair and a neatly trimmed beard. Crossing the room though, I could see that the two men were giving each other meaningful looks that suggested they were flirting. I diverted my course to stare at a painting rather than disturb them.

Unintentionally, I had fetched up against a chair. It was one of a pair tucked either side of a small table, so for lack of anything else to do, I sat down and settled in to pass a little time just watching the party. I would fetch another gin for myself when I felt inclined, but the party had been a mistake and I was going to have to ride it out without taking further part.

Across the room, Kristina reappeared and was talking to two girls when Melanie approached her carrying a drink in each hand. I saw her say something to Kristina, her head slightly bowed so that even from here I could see she was apologising. It worked; Melanie put the drinks down on a nearby counter as Kristina pulled her into a hug. Then I spotted Michael again. He was lurking just outside the open doors behind them. Had he slipped the security guards? Or simply jumped over the wall once they chucked him out? He was less than six feet away from Melanie and Kristina. Was he going to make another scene?

I thought that maybe I should get up and warn Melanie that he was back, she hadn't seen him, and his brow was knitted in anger. However, as I twitched to get up, I spotted Kristina's dad crossing the room. Maybe he had seen Michael and was already on his way to intercept him.

Then, Paul Rodriguez stepped in front of me, blocking my view so I couldn't see across the room. 'You destroyed me!' he shouted. 'I've got two viewers! You took my audience down to two!'

Kristina just laughed at him. 'You did that to yourself, Paul. What are you still doing here anyway? Isn't there a party for losers across town?' She delivered the line triumphantly, loving that she had been able to hurt him.

'I'm going to kill you,' he roared which was followed by gasps and screams as he lunged for her. His entourage grabbed him, hauling him away before he could get to her though he swore and spat insults and threats while she laughed in his face. I was bored with the spectacle of it all: young people showing off and acting in unnatural ways just to get attention. I started looking under the low table next to me to see if there might be a magazine. I wanted something to read to distract myself. Crouching to look under the low table, I could still hear the fading voice of Paul Rodriguez as his friends hauled him back. He was demanding they let him go and assuring everyone that he was fine and wouldn't do anything stupid. Having seemingly forgotten about him already, Kristina had gone back to jabbering nonsense into her camera as she moved between people in the crowd, all of whom seemed pleased to be given a chance to be seen with her. I glanced to see if Michael was still watching her but as she returned to where she had left Melanie, there was no longer any sign of him.

Disappointingly, there was nothing of interest beneath the table, so I looked about the room, hoping I might spot a bookshelf or even a room with a TV in it. None of those things presented themselves but cries of concern from across the room caught my attention. I had to hand it to Kristina; despite myself, I was constantly drawn to watch her.

Through the crowd I could see her. She was frozen, her expression confused as she stared at the drink in her hand. Everyone was staring directly at her, and Melanie was asking her what was wrong. But then the glass tumbled from her hand to smash on the floor and she collapsed to the marble tiles in a ragged heap.

Several people screamed in reaction, but no one moved. One of the ice cubes from her drink shot across the floor where it fetched up against my foot. It broke the spell for me, which galvanised me into motion just as Melanie knelt to shake her friend.

'Kristina!' she called, Barbie joining her a moment later as they tried to rouse her. 'Kristina!'

'What's happening?' asked her father, skidding to a stop on the low-friction floor. He looked horrified but he was staring at Melanie, not at his daughter when he said, 'What did you do?'

Barbie meantime was pulling Kristina's inert form into a better position so she could feel her pulse and start giving her treatment. Like all crew on the Aurelia, she was fully trained for first aid; there's no paramedic service in the middle of the Atlantic.

'Oh, my God,' she murmured. 'She's not breathing.'

I started moving faster, getting across the room as a sinking feeling filled my gut. Barbie ducked her head, ready to start mouth to mouth and I yelled to her, 'Stop!' The sound carried over the din of everyone else and caused her to look up. 'Don't,' I instructed. 'What if she's been poisoned?'

A sharp intake of breath bounced around the room and a fresh wave of chatter followed as Barbie stared back down at the women by her knees. Just then, an opaque white foam started to leak from the corner of Kristina's mouth. Barbie had one hand on her carotid artery, feeling her pulse. Her face gaunt, she looked up at me as her bottom lip wobbled. 'She's dead,' she said with a sob which elicited further cries and gasps from the guests. Even the music outside suddenly cut off. 'Someone poisoned her. Who would do that?' asked Barbie, her question barely audible as a tear leaked from one eye.

I had a few ideas.

I didn't bother to check Barbie's diagnosis; she was capable of determining if someone was alive or not. Instead, I looked around for the security guards. They were outside confronting Melanie's ex, Michael. Both men trying to corral him away from the building so they could eject him from the premises again.

'Stop them!' I yelled to the people outside the doors. All I got in response was blank expressions, so I went myself, stepping outside and getting within shouting distance. 'Guys!' I tried, but they were too caught up in their task. 'Guys!' this time with more volume, then I switched tactic and shouted, 'Hey, rentacops!' The insult got their attention, their heads swinging my way to see who they needed to deal with next. 'Gentlemen, please desist in removing that man. He needs to be kept here. There has been a murder.'

'What?' the security guards asked, their voices coming as one.

Hanging between them, Michael looked like he was going to faint, the colour had left his skin and as I took notice, he said 'I don't feel well.'

'Don't try any of that,' said the guard on the left. Both men in uniform had hold of an arm with one hand and Michael's shoulders with the other. They were acting tough but as Michael leaned forward and vomited, they both let go and danced back out of the way to avoid getting any on their shoes.

'Oh, I need to sit down,' said Michael as he staggered on wobbly legs to a low wall.

'How much did you have to drink, man?' asked the guard that had spoken before. He was the older of the two, but both looked to be in the mid to late thirties and out of shape. I guessed their heritage to be

Mexican, not that it made any difference, but I was getting worried about Michael and they were not. I wanted to get back inside to Barbie, but Michael looked like he needed treatment.

With one hand holding his head, Michael said, 'I'm just going to lie down for a bit.' But he didn't get to do that because he collapsed. Slumped as he was on the garden wall, he lost consciousness and pitched forward onto the ground.

'Do you two know CPR?' I snapped. Then said, 'Look after him, I'll be back soon.' I ducked quickly into the house again, dashing between the young party guests as they brainlessly gawped.

Inside, Jermaine had arrived next to Barbie. She was still holding Kristina and silently crying. There was a perimeter around the dead girl and those that were on the floor with her; the onlookers were too curious to go elsewhere and too horrified to come any closer. Jermaine stood when he saw me approaching. 'Madam, what can I do to assist?'

How was it that I was in charge? Everyone was looking at me as if I was the only adult in the room. But glancing around at the sea of faces that could remember their teens like it was yesterday (because it very nearly was!), I felt like maybe I was the only adult present. With a barely suppressed sigh, I said, 'Somebody please call 9-1-1. We need the police and the paramedics.' I realised my mistake as most of the people in the room pulled out their phones. At least someone would get through. Letting it go, I turned to Jermaine. 'Jermaine, please find something to cover the body and help Barbie to place her gently on the floor. We ought to preserve as much of the scene as we can.' While they did that, I looked for two large men; I had a task for them. Instantly, I spotted the quarter back Jermaine and Barbie had pointed out earlier. He was flanked by two men with upper arms the size of trashcans. Like almost everyone else in the room, they were watching me in mute fascination but looked terrified when I stared back at them. They glanced around hoping I was actually looking at someone else but didn't try to escape as I crossed the room.

'Gentleman, there must be close to two-hundred guests here. One of them is responsible for murdering Kristina. We need to keep everyone here until the police arrive. Can you go outside and stop people from leaving?' They nodded, looking thankful that I had given them an easy task and pushed through the crowd as they went in the direction of the front door. Finally, I turned my attention to everyone else, scanning around to see if I had their attention. Raising my voice, I said, 'I think Kristina was poisoned. If you have a drink that you are already drinking, you are probably safe. It would be safer to not drink them though but please do not throw them away because they may form useful evidence. Please place all the drinks on the bar where the police will be able to examine them.' Around the room there was a rush to be rid of whatever drink people were holding. The sound of glasses being put down echoed from all over as no one paid any attention to my request to put them on the bar. I kept quiet about Michael. I was worried he had been poisoned too, but more worried that the news would spread panic through the guests.

Looking toward the bar as I was, I saw the two handsome barmen there looked horrified, their expressions perhaps betraying concern that the star of the party had been poisoned by a drink one of them made.

I needed to check on Michael. I hadn't heard anything from outside since I left them out there to deal with him. Looking now, I could see that a crowd had formed so I went back outside again, shoving two men apart to squeeze my way through.

Michael was alive, I could tell straight away but he still looked deathly pale.

'Should we move him inside?' the elder guard asked.

I shook my head. 'The emergency services are on their way. They will be here soon enough.'

Then I heard a wail of disbelieving anguish coming from inside the house. The people forming a ring around Michael parted as I turned back toward the house. Coming through the open doors I saw that Kristina's mother was standing at the leading edge of the crowd around Barbie, her mouth hanging open in frozen shock. Then she fainted, the two young men either side of her stepping out of her way as she crumpled rather than catching her. There was a loud thump as her head hit the marble tile. I was getting angry with the overprivileged, uncaring, self-absorbed creatures surrounding me. 'You two!' I snapped, fixing the two young men with an accusing stare. 'Find a pillow for her head and take care of her until she comes around. When she does, I expect you to help her up and onto a sofa or a bed. Understood?'

They both nodded vigorously, like naughty boys being scolded by their mother and wishing they could be somewhere else. In the quiet of the room, I heard the distant wail of a cop car's siren and breathed a small sigh of relief. They would be here soon to sort out this mess and I would be able to go back to the ship.

As the sound of the siren grew louder, and Jermaine covered the body with a blanket he took from a sofa, the people in the room began to move away, conversation breaking out as they formed new clusters.

Looking down at the form beneath the blanket as Jermaine comforted Barbie a few feet away, I wondered who had killed her and why. One thing I was certain of: there was a killer somewhere among us.

'Oh, my goodness,' said Kristina's mother as she came to. Mary Blue had grown old like we all do. I wasn't sure how old she was, but she had to have a decade on me and be in her sixties now. However, unlike my blonde hair, which was shot through with grey, hers looked like she had borrowed it from a model on a shampoo bottle. Also, her face was devoid of the lines and wrinkles I expected to see on a woman her age; no doubt the result of some expensive nipping and tucking. The two men I had yelled at were both on their knees and taking an arm each to help her sit up. 'Oh, my. Oh, my baby,' she wailed, staring at the covered lump ten feet away.

Melanie and Barbie went to her, wrapping her into a hug as they all wept. Jermaine stood like a sentinel over the body. Not that anyone was trying to get to it, but he had taken it upon himself to stay with the girl until the coroner arrived.

The sirens reached a crescendo and fell silent; the cops had arrived. My head was filling with questions that demanded answers. There were already parts of this puzzle that didn't fit.

The Cops

I didn't go to the door; it wasn't my house and I wasn't in charge despite the general consensus of the party goers. Instead, I went across to the bar where the two barmen were still looking shocked by the turn of events.

'Did you bring all the drinks with you today?' I asked.

Glumly, the man on the right nodded. 'It's our business. This was going to get us massive exposure. Catering Kristina Khymera's party would have got us stacks more business; we were really getting there. Now what do we do?'

'Steady, Brad. A woman died. We can't focus on our problems.' His friend had a clearer sense of right and wrong.

Brad wasn't convinced though. 'She died drinking one of our drinks, Matt. The cops are going to crawl all over us, and no one is going to hire the two guys that killed Kristina. I've got everything invested in this business. I don't have rich parents I can fall back on.'

'What?' Matt was not pleased with his colleague's attitude. As the two barmen got chest to chest, I gave up; I would talk to them later.

From the raised mezzanine that looked down onto the room from the entrance lobby above, two uniformed cops and two men in suits were now visible. Two EMTs with heavy bags over their shoulders raced around them, coming to the top of the stairs they looked around for someone to tell them where they were needed.

For the first time in the last fifteen minutes, someone else showed some gumption. One of the security guards had come to the doors at the back of the house. 'Over here,' he called, waving his right arm to make himself visible. 'We have an unconscious man in the garden.' The paramedics swept down the stairs and through the guests to follow him outside.

At the top of the stairs stood the uniformed cops. A man and a woman. They were both young, maybe late twenties but no older. Of the two detectives that flanked them, one looked to be about the same age as the pair in uniform but the other one had to be close to retirement age by my estimation. The younger of the two came to the edge of the glass balustrade and raised his voice to get the attention of the room. He wore a sharp suit that looked tailored, his appearance more that of a politician than a man working in homicide. Maybe he was one of those cops that planned to go all the way and then use his career as a springboard for office. 'Ladies and gentlemen, I am Detective Davis, this is Detective Sergeant Washington.' He indicated the elder man in his grey suit. 'We need to empty this room and we need to speak with each and every one of you. The...'

'It was her!' a woman's voice rang out to cut off what the detective had been saying. I couldn't see who had spoken but the crowd soon parted, people standing near to her distancing themselves quickly. 'I saw her hand Kristina the drink.' She was pointing directly at Melanie. 'And she wanted to get back at Kristina for shouting at her earlier.'

'What?' Melanie was still on the marble floor with Barbie and Kristina's mum. 'I didn't poison her,' she replied, her denial sounding hollow in the face of the accusation and the room-full of people staring at her.

'I saw you,' the woman retorted like she was stating facts and performing a public service.

The cops were coming down the stairs already, people at the bottom moving away to allow them access. The young detective in the lead pointed his finger at Melanie. 'I think we had better start with you,' he said.

Melanie got to her feet as they approached, leaving the grieving mother with Barbie. The elder detective remained silent as the younger one took charge again. He gave instructions to the uniformed cops, telling them to find him a room in which he could conduct an interview and to call in additional officers: they needed to speak to everyone at the party and get phone numbers and addresses for everyone. Then he addressed the crowd, 'Ladies and gentlemen, we will try to make this as painless as possible. I ask for your cooperation while we conduct our investigation.'

Detective Davis didn't hang around, he was leaving the room, heading toward a corridor that led deeper into the house where the lady cop had already found a suitable room. Meekly, Melanie went with him when he told her to.

'How long until we can leave?' asked a voice from the crowd.

The seasoned detective spoke for the first time, making a face that made me think he had been asked that question a lot of times before. He said, 'I think you should all make yourselves comfortable. Unless someone comes forward to confess, this is likely to take a few hours. Most of you will be interviewed by uniformed officers and will be free to go once we have a statement from you.' Then he turned to follow where his younger colleague had gone, and the uniformed cops started to organise the people in the room.

The lady cop went to Mary Blue as her male counterpart came to examine the body for himself. With cops here, any role I had briefly fulfilled was now complete so, like everyone else, I had to wait my turn to be interviewed and released. Looking about, I saw that the chair I had been sitting in when Kristina dropped dead was vacant, so I made my way to it and was about to sit when I spotted a small pool of water on the floor. It was from the ice cube that had shot across the floor from her smashed glass.

The barmen weren't serving ice cubes though.

The observation just popped into my head uninvited, demanding I pay attention to it. Frowning at the inconsistency, I walked back to the bar where Brad and Matt had stopped bickering but were now standing at opposite ends of the counter looking decidedly acrimonious. They saw me coming but neither moved.

'Chaps, have you served any ice cubes?' I asked.

The block of ice they had been chipping ice from was melting slowly just where it had been previously. Matt saw me looking at it and said, 'No, we just use shaved ice. Ice cubes are so gauche.'

Brad had something to say as well, 'Ice cubes are cheap, Matt,' he snapped. 'We could have added two percent profit on top if we made ice cubes from tap water at home and brought them with us. Gauche? Your giant block of ice impresses no one.'

Matt's face turned angry as his fists balled, so I quickly jumped back in before either man could say anything else. 'There were ice cubes in Kristina's drink. If you don't have ice cubes, how did they get there?'

Matt and Brad weren't listening though. Despite my presence, they had elected to throw insults at each other that looked likely to end only when they upgraded to punching one another. Their language was getting quite colourful, so I left them and went in search of the detectives.

Jermaine appeared by my side as I crossed the room. 'Madam, is there anything I can do to assist you at this time?' When I paused to look at him, he said, 'You appear to be engaged in detective work, madam. I recognise the expression you pull when you have a mystery to unravel.'

I didn't know that I had an expression that went with solving mysteries. I would have to check in the mirror later. While my brain whirred at full speed, I realised that I did have a job for Jermaine. 'Can you locate Kristina's father?' I asked. 'He was here when she collapsed, but I haven't seen him since. I'm sure he is distraught but no doubt his wife could use his support and the cops will want to speak with him as he was very close when it happened and may have seen something. Also, I am mildly worried his absence might mean he is...' I made a universally recognised gesture for hanging oneself but did so surreptitiously so no one else would see.

With a curt nod of understanding, Jermaine said, 'I will track him down, madam.' He departed through the crowd as I resumed my search for the detectives. I had seen which door they went through, but the house was vast, so once I too went through it, I was faced with too many options including, not one, but two staircases.

There were doors on either side of the corridor I was in which carried on to reach what looked to be a central hub from which more spokes branched off. Since I had no way of knowing where they had gone, I grabbed a door handle and opened it. 'Okay, that's a toilet,' I said to myself then moved to the next door and tried again.

This time there were occupants in the room, a young couple who had left the party to spend some time, um... getting to know one another. A scream lit the air. 'Get out!' yelled the woman as she let go of the man's hair to grab a nearby object. It turned out to be a vase. As I quickly shut the door again, I heard it smash on the other side.

Now I was wondering how many other doors might have surprises behind them. I didn't get to find out though, because a door opened behind me and the young detective stuck his head out.

I was right in front of his face. 'Hey,' he said, 'can you get one of the uniformed officers for me, please?'

'I was looking for you,' I said in response to his request. 'I think the poison, whatever it was, was delivered in an ice cube. The barmen are using shaved ice,' I began to explain, but Detective Davis flapped his hand in front of my face.

'I don't have time for amateur hour, toots. Don't waste your time. We already got the killer. We'll have a confession within the hour. I'll get the uniform myself.'

'Evidence? What evidence?' asked Barbie. I guess she had seen me leave and decided to follow.

'Who are you?' asked Detective Davis, clearly surprised by the pretty blonde lady he now faced.

Barbie folded her arms, feeling defensive and basically giving herself a hug. 'I'm a friend of Melanie's. She and I went to school with Kristina.'

'Well, I hear that the two of them got into quite the argument not less than thirty minutes before she died. Kristina made her break up with her boyfriend, didn't she?'

Barbie kept quiet.

'Come on,' he said with a sneer. 'You can tell me. Kristina was a bitch that got her own way, bossed everyone around and made millions doing it. Your friend,' he said with quote fingers in the air, 'knew it was only a matter of time before Kristina fired her for good, so she got her revenge in early. I will need to talk to you for that matter, *friend of the suspect*,' he said with more quote fingers. 'A crime like this; she's bound to have an accomplice.' The unpleasant cop in his great suit turned to go looking for a uniformed cop, but he had a parting remark, 'Be sure you don't go anywhere, blondie.' Then he walked away, shouting loudly to draw attention like he was the most important person in the house.

I took Barbie's hand. 'Barbie, we need to ask ourselves who would benefit from her death. Let's head back to the main room and work through this.' As we walked, I told her about the ice cube and asked if she had seen anything; had anyone got close enough to spike Kristina's drink? I had no idea if Melanie had killed Kristina or not, but Barbie believed she was innocent and that was good enough for me.

Clues

Back in the main room there were more cops than there had been when I left. I counted no fewer than eight officers in uniform. Each had on blue prophylactic gloves and most were talking to the party guests as they built up a picture of who had seen what. The body was shielded from view by a screen, but moving to an oblique angle, I could see a man in a cheap suit was kneeling to examine it. The back of his scalp was visible where grey hair was getting very thin on top and looked to be overdue a cut in general. His suit was a little crumpled from the heat and from being in a car no doubt, and he was thickset as if the years had unkindly added a pound or two with each birthday.

A younger man, dressed more causally, but with a badge tucked over his belt, was taking photographs. As I approached, he took the camera away from his face. 'Stay back please, ma'am.'

Ignoring his instruction, I asked as I pointed to Kristina, 'What's that powder?' On Kristina's shoulder was what looked like a faint, white handprint. Someone had touched her, and they had white powder on their hands when they did it. Was it cocaine?

The man moved to block me, calling across the room to one of the uniforms. He wanted us moved away but the cop was busy already. I waved my hand in a gesture that let him know we were leaving, and he said once more, 'Stay back, ma'am. I'll have you removed if you come over here again.'

I nodded, my brain spinning once again as I committed what I had seen to memory. I wasn't going to get a better look at her, though it horrified me that I wanted to. Barbie was right behind me, waiting for me to work some magic and find a way to prove Melanie's innocence. Whatever I had been thinking vanished though as a shout came from outside. One of the EMTs was calling for the CSI guy's attention.

'See what they want, will you, Robbie?' asked the balding coroner in his tired suit. He didn't bother to look up from what he was doing, and the younger man offered no response as he put his camera down. I moved to one side so I could see and watched as the younger CSI chap went outside. There was no one to stop me, so I took Barbie's hand and dragged her with me as I followed him.

'What've you got?' he asked the EMT. The pair of medics were alone now. The crowd of guests that had surrounded Michael when they arrived were long gone, moved away by the police no doubt. Michael was hooked up to a machine that was monitoring his pulse and blood oxygen. His polo shirt had been cut open to expose his chest and there were pads stuck in several spots each with a wire going into the machine. On his face was a mask feeding him oxygen.

The EMT that had called for assistance held up a plastic bag, like an evidence bag, in which I saw a small, orange tub; the type you get pills in from the pharmacy. 'This is most likely the source of his distress. He is showing signs of cyanide poisoning which he could have got from handling the pills, if that's what they are. It was tucked into his jacket pocket.'

'Cyanide? We'll have to test this back at the lab, but if these are cyanide pills,' he held the bag up to the light and shook it to move the pills around in the tub, 'then it's more than enough to kill the victim.'

Barbie put her hand to her mouth and gasped, drawing attention to our presence which made the CSI guy Robbie frown in consternation when he turned and saw us behind him.

'We were just going,' I said before he could call a cop to move us along.

Back inside the house, Barbie leaned in close to whisper in my ear as we walked, 'Oh, my God, Patty, Michael's the killer.'

It certainly looked that way. 'Barbie can you call Jermaine and see how he is getting on?' I asked.

She said, 'Sure,' and fished around in her clutch to get her phone. 'Oh, it's dead.' I turned to look at her, my attention caught between what she was trying to tell me and another two CSI guys who were on their knees near to where Kristina had dropped her glass. 'My phone battery died,' Barbie said with a sigh. 'I guess I forgot to check it this morning.' She looked about the room. 'Patty, I'm going to find somewhere to charge this, won't be a moment.'

As she darted away, I went a few paces closer to the CSI guys. The cops were still filtering all the party guests out of the room, so I couldn't have any more than a couple of minutes before I too would be escorted out.

On the floor the CSI guys were gathering fragments of Kristina's broken glass into a tray but as I tried to get close, a young cop with short black hair blocked my way. 'Sorry, ma'am. Please join the others, it is not possible to leave at this time.' He thought I was heading upstairs to the front door and freedom, and I didn't correct him. I didn't pay him much attention either because I could see one of the CSI guys holding a large fragment of glass up to the light.

'Hey, John, how many victims have we got again?' he asked of his colleague.

The other man was using a pair of tweezers to pick a tiny fragment from the tile and had his head as low as he could, trying to see other fragments that wouldn't show up if he looked directly down at them. He held up one finger, the middle one as it so happened, though it was probably nothing more than banter passing between two people with horrible jobs. 'Just one, Henry. Just one.'

'Yeah,' said Henry, still holding the piece of glass up toward the sun. 'Then why do I have two shades of lipstick on this glass?'

'Hmm?' replied John, now interested and looking at what Henry had. 'Let me see that.' He moved in close to his partner, his lips pursed and his eyes squinting to see. 'Yup, that's two shades of lipstick right there. There's enough cyanide in this to drop a rhino though, so whoever that lipstick belongs to didn't drink from this glass.' Then he noticed me watching him from just a few feet away and shouted to the cop, 'Hey, can you do your job and keep people back?'

The cop muttered something but locked eyes with me. His expression was easy to understand: go away. I took a step back just as Barbie touched my shoulder. 'What do we do next, Patty?' she asked.

'Ladies,' a voice rang out. It was the female officer that had arrived in the first wave of cops. She had had two fingers crooked at us, demanding we come to her. 'I need you to join the others now. We are sealing this room.' Her tone was professionally board but polite. It hadn't taken them long to get organised; ten minutes or so to get in, set up, erect a screen around Kristina and move all the guests to another part of the house. I was duly impressed with their efficiency but couldn't stop myself from worrying that neither Melanie nor Michael were guilty.

As we followed the lady cop from the room, I took one final look around, but the door shut behind me as she led us further into the house. We passed the door to the room the detectives were in, around a corner and into another large room that had panoramic windows looking out across the garden and LA beyond. It had a broad, pitched glass roof like an orangery one might find on a country house back in England. It was another big space, but it felt cramped because it was filled with people from the party.

'We can't just stay in here, Patty,' said Barbie. She was biting her lip and looking around to see what the cops were doing.

'I want to talk to her parents,' I replied. 'Do you know where they might be?'

Barbie gave my question some thought. 'Her mother might have gone to her room. She isn't here so that is the next place I would look.'

'What about her father?' I asked. Jermaine hadn't reported back so must be having more trouble finding him than expected. 'Oh, hold on. I'm going to call Jermaine and see how he is getting on.'

The call connected straight away; his deep voice easy to recognise. 'Madam, may I presume you are calling for an update on my task?'

'You may.'

'Then I can report that I have not yet located the gentleman in question though I have seen him. I was not able to follow directly as two police officers came upstairs looking for any party goers that might have absconded to a bedroom. By the time they passed, I had lost him again.'

'Did he seem to be in distress?' I asked.

'I was not able to get close enough to tell, madam. Should I return to you, or do you wish for me to continue searching?'

I considered the question for a moment. The police could find Kristina's father, I could even prompt them to the task, but Jermaine was bound to find him shortly and something was amiss with the clues I had found: the ice cube for a start. It had to mean something. Then there was the powder handprint on Kristina's top. The CSI guys would not be so clumsy as to contaminate the evidence, so it had to be from someone that handled her as she fell. That was a small subset of people, but I didn't see how any of them could be the killer. Then there was Michael. Was he so dumb that he had poisoned himself while he was poisoning Kristina? I struggled to believe it. Nothing was adding up, so I wanted Jermaine to remain in play, so to speak, not be stuck in here with us waiting to be processed and sent home by the cops. Reaching a decision, I said, 'No, Jermaine, please keep on with the task for now and let me know when you locate him.'

'Very good, madam.' I ended the call and put the phone away in my handbag. When I looked up, Barbie touched my arm.

'There's no one watching the door over there, Patty. Shall we find Kristina's mom?' Barbie was pointing to a different door to the one we came in. I didn't think we were prisoners, but the police had a task to perform which would be easier with all the people kept in one place so why was this exit unmanned? Following Barbie's lead, we found that the door led to a toilet which was why the cops were not preventing people from going through it. As a mean of escape, it was no use to us. However, Barbie's knowledge of the house proved helpful when she whispered, 'There's another way out of that bathroom.'

She told me that when she was a child there had been a games room on the other side where she had played with the other young girls. The toilet had doors so it could be accessed from both sides, or at least sort of. She didn't expand on what that meant but did express hope that they hadn't remodelled and closed it off in the intervening years. We waited for the occupant in the toilet to come out, the sound of the flush preceding the sound of the latch and a young Mexican man with a stubbly chin opened the door. He jumped when he saw the two ladies outside waiting to get in.

'Oh, um. You might want to give it a second, ladies,' he warned. But I wasn't of a mind to hang about. I should have heeded his words though because the smell assailing our nostrils once we were inside the toilet was something else.

'Ewww, that's nasty!' exclaimed Barbie while covering her face and holding her breath. She crossed the room to another door which I would have guessed held a boiler. I was wrong as behind the door was a sauna and that had another door to it that led into the games room.

'What do you know? The old pool table is still here,' she said, a brief moment of nostalgia catching her by surprise. Shaking herself free of the memory, she said, 'Her mom's room used to be the big one at the back of the house, so I hope it still is because otherwise there are a lot of rooms to search.'

Thankfully, Kristina's mum hadn't seen a need to move rooms in the last few years, so when we got upstairs, we could hear her in her bedroom but the door to the room was being guarded by a female police officer.

'Ladies, you are not supposed to be roaming the house. Please return to the officers downstairs so they can process and release you.' The woman's face and demeanour meant business. It was clear she was a seasoned professional and not to be messed with.

However, Barbie said, 'I am a childhood friend of Kristina and have known Mrs Wilshaw since I started school. It sounds like she needs some comfort.'

If the lady cop was going to argue, any thought of doing so died when Mrs Wilshaw's voice echoed out through the door. 'Barbie, is that you?'

The uniformed officer inclined her head; *go on then.*

Inside the bedroom, we found Kristina's mother gently sobbing on her bed. Barbie knocked softly on the door as she went it, calling out, 'Mrs Wilshaw? It's Barbie. I just wanted to check how you are doing.'

The crumpled form on the bed didn't even look up. She blew her nose though. The loud trumpeting sound of misery she made struck home the death we had witnessed. I had been so focused on trying to work out what had happened, I had almost forgotten that a woman had died. Then she turned her face upward to look at the woman she had known as a girl. 'Barbie, dear, have you seen my husband anywhere?'

'Um, no. Hasn't he been with you?' she asked in surprise.

'I haven't seen him since Kristina...' she gulped back a sob as she said her daughter's name. I couldn't imagine the pain she must be feeling but the father must be feeling it too. Had he taken off to deal with his grief alone? It was odd that he wasn't with her, but then rational thought and actions probably didn't apply at a time like this. I hoped Jermaine would find him soon lest he hurt himself.

Barbie had joined the woman on her bed and was stroking her hair, trying to give her comfort. I kept respectfully quiet for several minutes, hating that I had come here to ask her questions but knowing that I had to for Melanie's sake.

After five or more minutes ticked by, I moved into Barbie's eyeline, catching her attention. I didn't really want to interrupt, but I didn't want to wait either. 'Mrs Wilshaw,' Barbie whispered.

'Oh, sweetie, you can call me, Mary. We are both adults now,' the aging singer managed between sniffs.

'Mary,' Barbie started again, 'there is a lady here to see you. She wants to ask you a few questions.'

'About my Kristina?' she asked, lifting her head to see if there really was another person in the room.

'Yes,' I replied, giving her my most sympathetic smile. 'The police may be reacting to misleading evidence.'

'They have Melanie in custody,' added Barbie. 'They think she did it.'

'Melanie? Why would Melanie kill Kristina?' Mary Blue asked as she laid her head back down.

'She wouldn't,' Barbie assured her. 'That's why we need to work out who would. The detectives think Melanie was acting out of jealousy because Kristina was so successful and because the two of them had an argument just before... just before it happened,' Barbie stuttered, correcting herself mid-sentence rather articulate Kristina's death.

On the bed, Kristina's mother blew her nose again.

'What do you know about Kristina breaking up Melanie and her boyfriend?' I asked.

Mary Blue raised her head to look at me. 'I know she thought she was doing the right thing. She loved Melanie. Even when they were little girls, Kristina always looked out for her.' Her statement made me remember my own childhood friend. Maggie had always been there for me, through breakups and miscarriages she was my rock to cling to, right up until she slept with my husband and changed the course of my life. Were Kristina and Melanie the same or different to Maggie and me?

Rather than voice my thoughts, I nodded my understanding and pushed on. 'Mrs Wilshaw, do you know of anyone that would want to hurt Kristina, or would benefit from her death?'

My question appeared to reopen the wound as Mrs Wilshaw let out a shuddering sigh and didn't answer for several seconds. I didn't have to prompt her though, after a short while, she blew her nose and wiped her eyes and forced herself into a seated position on the bed, Barbie slid out of her way as she did. 'I don't know, really. There are other online personalities that have been trying to steal her crown of course, but none of them have ever threatened her to my knowledge. That loathsome Paul Rodriguez might talk big, but he is a nobody and I can't see him growing a pair big enough to kill someone.' She turned her attention to Barbie. 'You knew her Barbara. Can you think of anyone that would hurt her?'

Barbie shook her head slowly and deliberately. 'Kristina was loved by most people. I can't think of anyone that would want her dead.'

'What about someone from her past?' I asked. Are there any skeletons in her closet? Old boyfriends that might wish ill of her? What about Michael, Melanie's ex? He seemed angry about Kristina's interference.' And he was carrying cyanide pills in his jacket.

'He was angry,' Barbie agreed. 'I don't know him though, only that Kristina advised Melanie to dump him and she did.'

I frowned as the next question formed. 'Why?'

'That was Kristina's skill. She succeeded in giving advice on life and relationships and stuff because she could tell what people were like. She had some kind of natural ability, that was how she got popular and it grew and grew until she live-streamed almost everything...' Barbie's face took on a glazed look. She was thinking about something and focusing on it rather than speaking. Then, her expression unfroze, and she started moving toward the door. 'Patty, we need to check something.'

Mrs Wilshaw looked a little startled as Barbie left her bedroom without another word, leaving me standing at the end of her bed and feeling awkward.

'Patty, come on!' yelled Barbie from somewhere outside, her voice already starting to sound distant.

Mrs Wilshaw was staring at me, her expression bewildered. I opened my mouth to excuse myself, but she said, 'Go! Go, find out who killed my daughter!'

I all but ran from the room, getting out into the upper landing area just in time to see Barbie's blonde hair vanish down the stairs. The bored lady cop by the bedroom door pulled it shut again but paid neither of us any mind as we sped back downstairs. Barbie called for me to hurry up again, but Barbie isn't the kind of person you can keep up with. Serious athletes would struggle to keep up with her as she appeared to be part gazelle, part cheetah and part super-fit gym bunny. I found her though, waiting for me at the bottom of the stairs. It wasn't the stairs we had gone up though and we had come back out near the room the detectives were in with Melanie.

'What's going on?' I asked, a little out of breath.

'I needed my phone,' Barbie replied. 'I put it here to charge.' She was poised with it in her palm, waiting for it to come to life. 'Yay!' she squeaked as the screen switched from dead and black to colourful and lively. 'I suddenly realised I could dial into Kristina's feed and take it back to view it again.'

'You can do that?' I asked, once again showing off my lack of knowledge when it came to modern technology.

Barbie's focus was on her phone, her fingers doing things to the touchscreen to make it obey her. She said, 'Sure,' absentmindedly answering my question as she fiddled. 'Here.' She showed me the screen, which was now filled with Kristina's face, frozen in time, but halfway through saying something so she was pulling a very odd face while staring upwards at the camera held above her head. 'The live feed gets saved as one-hour blocks so we could, in theory, look at any of her broadcasts since the very start. This is the very last segment.'

She pressed the play icon on the screen and Kristina's face came to life, her voice booming out loudly enough to attract the attention of a cop that had thus far been ignoring us. 'Oops,' said Barbie. 'I had it turned up to listen to music this morning.' The volume died back to an acceptable level as the footage played. 'I need to forward it a bit,' she said, fiddling with the screen again to leap ahead ten minutes.

'What are you ladies doing?' asked the cop. He was African American and handsome with a strong jaw. He was athletic too, with defined muscle showing from the cuffs of his sleeves. 'Shouldn't you be in the orangery with everyone else?' He had crossed the room to ask the question but saw what Barbie was looking at and instantly understood its significance. 'Does that show who poisoned Kristina?' he asked, his voice excited.

'We don't know yet,' Barbie replied quietly as she stared at the tiny screen. Now three of us were crowded around it, intently studying what the screen showed. Kristina had a style of filming that would make some people sick. The tiny camera on the end of her selfie-stick stayed in focus but it moved around a lot, tracking her as she talked to it and to other people.

Barbie said, 'I need to go forward a little more,' and did the thing with her finger again. It leaped forward once more, this time restarting when Kristina was belittling Paul Rodriguez. We watched it through, heard him threaten her and then had to watch her die again as she lifted the glass and downed the contents. When she hit the floor, all three of us sucked in a breath that we had been holding: It was hard to watch.

'Patty, did you see anyone go near the drink?' asked Barbie.

I shook my head. 'The drink isn't in shot most of the time.' That was Kristina's style; the camera never stayed in one place for long.

The young cop asked, 'Can we see it again but with the volume off? It might help to focus just on sight and not sound.' Barbie nodded and took the footage back. As she pressed play, the cop said, 'Stop. Who is that right there?' He was pointing to a man on the screen lurking just inside the door behind Kristina. He wore an angry scowl on his face, and he had something in his hands.

'That's Michael,' I supplied. 'Melanie's ex-boyfriend.'

'Ok, let it play, but I want to see what he is holding, so stop if it comes on screen, okay?'

'Okay,' said Barbie as she let the footage run again. We watched it through three times, just to be sure, but it wasn't a small orange plastic pill bottle he was carrying, it looked more like he had an egg in his hand. Had he planned to splat an egg on her head? The focus wasn't sharp enough to tell what it was though, only that moments before Kristina died, Michael had been sneaking up behind her.

'That's the man they found carrying the cyanide pills,' the young cop stated. 'I need to show this to the detectives.' He took two steps and knocked on the door to the room they were in.

When it opened a few seconds later, it was the younger of the two detectives that stuck his face out. 'What?' he demanded looking impatient.

'I have something I think you should see,' replied the young officer, not even slightly cowed by the detective's attitude. 'I think we have an accomplice.'

Now the detective was interested but Barbie said, 'What? No! Melanie doesn't have an accomplice because she didn't do it!'

'Oh yeah?' Detective Davis stopped to lock eyes with Barbie. 'Tell me then, Miss...'

'Berkeley,' she supplied, filling in the gap he had left for her to answer, 'Barbara Berkeley.'

'Well, Miss Barbara Berkeley, tell me why your friend has twenty thousand dollars in cash in her handbag.' Detective Davis continued staring at her, daring her to have an answer while always watching her for facial cues. 'No answer, huh? I'll tell you what I think, Miss Berkeley. I think your friend paid someone to kill her boss and the twenty thousand is the other half of the money to be paid when the job is done.' Then he turned his attention away from Barbie to focus on the cop. 'Now you say you've found an accomplice?'

The cop nodded as he started to explain, 'The guy they found with the cyanide in his jacket. The one that had a mild case of cyanide poisoning that is already on his way to the hospital. He can be seen sneaking up on the victim right before she picks up the drink and gets poisoned. He is clearly holding something in his hands.'

'Something? What something?' Davis demanded.

'It looks like an egg,' I answered quickly. Detective Davis glanced at me, one eyebrow raised. 'An egg?'

'The footage doesn't show what it is,' the cop admitted as Davis pinched his nose with his thumb and forefinger in a display of frustration. 'But...'

'Oh, there's a but? You have a but for me?' Davis was an obnoxious man that I was finding it hard to tolerate. Had it been me he was talking to, I would have walked away, but the young officer had more patience or perhaps knew he would get an apology later because he said, 'The man is your suspect's boyfriend.'

The detective's eyes lit up. He turned his head slightly to speak over his shoulder as he held the door behind him open a crack. 'Washington, we just found the smoking gun. Let's take her downtown.' He let the door shut. 'She won't talk without a lawyer present anyway. But there'll be a confession soon enough.' He even started whistling as he walked away.

'What do we do, Patty?' asked Barbie, her voice quiet.

I had been thinking while everyone else was talking. None of the clues made sense. If I placed myself in Melanie's shoes and tried to play the murder through from her perspective as if I wanted Kristina dead, it still didn't make sense. In fact, none of the scenarios made sense until I switched my focus completely and asked a different question. Then, seeing the possibility of the answer for the first time, I smiled a wry smile and said, 'We let them make fools of themselves, then present them with the real killer.'

Barbie was mystified by my answer, but I couldn't tell her much more yet because I hadn't worked it all out. There had been something itching away at the back of my head ever since I spotted the ice cube by my foot.

I took her hand and walked her along the corridor we were in and back into the orangery where most of the party guests were still visible. I spotted four uniformed cops in the room, going between the different groups still asking questions, recording answers and getting contact details for later. It felt like the guests had been retained for ages, but when I checked my watch it was still barely more than an hour since Kristina drank the killer cocktail.

Checking that no one could overhear me, I asked, 'Have you had a missed call from Jermaine?'

'No,' replied Barbie. 'Where did you send him? He's been gone ages.'

'I asked him to find Kristina's father. I'll give him a little longer before I call him.' I knew my butler to be diligent and very capable of looking after himself, so I had no concerns about him goofing off or running into trouble. Nevertheless, I was beginning to worry. 'There must be other footage of the party. Paul Rodriguez was filming even if no one was watching, but I think some of his friends had their phones out too.'

Barbie and I scanned around the room, but if Paul Rodriguez was still here, we couldn't see him. 'I guess he was one of the lucky ones that got released already,' said Barbie. 'I would have thought they would keep him here seeing as how he threatened to kill her.'

'Maybe they did. Maybe they have him and his crew in another one of the rooms like Melanie. Will his stuff be online?' I asked hopefully.

'It will only take a second to check.' Barbie pulled her phone from her bag and played around with it. Squinting at the screen, she said, 'No, it's not here. It says content removed.'

'Content removed?' What does that mean? Would he have taken it down out of respect for Kristina's dignity?'

Barbie gave me a look that told me I was way off the mark. 'More likely that he thought it a good idea to not show Kristina making him look like a fool and then him threatening to kill her right before she dropped dead.'

I guess that made sense. 'We need to see if his footage shows anything. We need to get hold of it. Do you know anyone that would have his number?' Then I realised it would be written down if he had been released. 'Hold on.' I went to the nearest cop. 'Has Paul Rodriguez been released already?'

The man gave me a patient look as if deciding whether he was in a mood to answer questions instead of ask them, but reaching a decision, he glanced down at his paperwork for a few seconds to check the names. 'Yes,' he replied without looking at me. 'About ten minutes ago. I would imagine he has left the property by now.'

'Did you take down his number? I need to speak with him.'

This time the cop gave me a sideways look. 'Hey lady, if I had a person's number, do you really think I would give it to you?'

I swung around to speak with Barbie. 'I guess they didn't see him as a likely suspect despite the threat and Detective Davis is too blinkered to consider anyone else. We have to get his number.'

'Okay,' said Barbie. Then she climbed on a chair to make herself two feet taller and shouted, 'Who has Paul Rodriguez's number?' The question was accompanied by her doe-eyed winning smile which had an instant impact on all the men in the room, including the cop I had just been talking to.

'Hey lady,' he said again. 'You should get her to ask for things in the future.' His comment was followed by a ripping noise as he tore a strip of paper off his notepad. 'That's the number he gave,' he said as he leaned in front of me to hand the scrap of paper to Barbie. 'The number below it labelled Chuck is my number. I'll be free tonight.' He gave Barbie a cheeky wink and went back to speaking with the person he was supposed to be talking to.

Oh, to be twenty-two and flawlessly pretty.

Barbie smiled at me and said, 'Well, that worked. I'll call him.'

'Let's go in the bathroom. There's less noise there and I want to hear what he says.'

Thirty seconds later, in the bathroom that had this time not been made inhospitable by a young man's diet, Barbie copied the number into her phone. 'Try facetime?' I asked, taking the advice of the cop. If Paul saw Barbie's face, he might be more inclined to do as she was going to ask.

The phone made a small chiming noise and there was Paul's face. 'Hello,' he said before he had even looked at who was at the other end.

'Hello again, Paul, It's, Barbie,' said Barbie. 'I hope you remember me from the party. Do you have time to speak with me?' Her voice had dropped an octave and was coming out hushed and breathless like she was making a dirty phone call.

He was already smitten. I could tell by his goofy smile. 'Wh... what is it you want to talk about?' he stuttered.

'I work in PR,' lied Barbie smoothly. 'I saw what Kristina did this afternoon, and I think you can use it to find millions of viewers. You have footage from the party, right? Footage that shows the moment she collapsed?'

'Yeah. I can't release that though. I took it down as soon as I realised what had happened to her.'

'Because you had just threatened her, right?'

'Well, yeah.' He was answering her questions but had no idea where she was leading him.

'Think about it then. Kristina is gone. Nothing will bring her back but there is a sudden vacuum and you can fill it. You have compelling footage that everyone will want to see. More than that though, you have a duty to complete her work and show her final moments. She lived her whole life on screen, it is only fitting that she ends it there too.' Barbie's voice wobbled slightly as she talked about her friend's death, but she kept it together and Paul didn't notice. She was doing a great job!

'Really?' Paul's tone was hopeful now, excited at the prospect of scoring big.

'You could be the one that shows Kristina's final moments and if you do it right, by showing the world how real you are by not adding filters or editing to take out the parts where she makes you look bad or where you threaten her, the phone will start ringing and it will never stop. I'd be willing to bet you could be on TV within the week.' That sold it, I could see the dollar signs dancing in his eyes as he considered the possibilities.

'Wait,' he said, crashing back to reality. 'Why are you telling me this? What's in it for you? You weren't interested when I spoke to you at the party.'

Barbie smiled demurely into the phone and bit her lip as if she was working up to saying something that was embarrassing. 'I didn't know who you were then, Paul. I didn't know who you were about to be. I'm single, Paul, and let's just say I don't want to be. I think it might be fun to date the hottest winner in town, so I get to help with your success while you get to help me undress.' The end of the sentence came out as a teased breath. I could almost hear his trousers tightening.

'Okay. Yeah, okay. I'm going to get the footage back up now. Unedited like you said. Should I add a voiceover or something, explain what was happening so people have a clear context of why I am showing it?'

'No, lover. Just wait for the phone calls, it will be so much more magnanimous for you if they ask the questions you haven't answered. You've got my number. Make sure you call it later.' She bit her lip again and waved him goodbye, then pressed the button to end the call.

I took a step back and said, 'Wow,' while I gave her a short round of applause. 'That was amazing. You totally just wrecked his life though, you know that.'

'Yup. Going to have to throw my phone overboard too.'

'You really think he's stupid enough to put the footage back up?' I asked, though I was sure I already knew the answer: he was. I doubted there were many men that wouldn't do as Barbie asked.

'Let's see, shall we?' Barbie had her phone in her hand still and was fiddling with the screen again to bring up the app. 'Oh, my word, here it is,' she gasped as it started to play. We were watching a familiar scene;

one I had seen live as it happened and then twice through in a recording. It was different each time though, the angles changed to give a different view but once again, Barbie whizzed through most of it to get to the final scenes. Just as she had before, she turned the volume off so we could better study what we were watching.

Paul's camera was focused on him of course, not on Kristina, though even with the sound muted I could tell he was being unpleasant about her as he talked to his imaginary audience. I was ready to bet he would have an audience soon; it would be one that was ready to lynch him though so I had to hope he would come to his senses and take the footage back down before too many people saw it.

We reached the moment he realised his meagre audience was gone and Kristina had trounced him. His camera angle swung to take her in as no doubt his voice continued to berate her. I saw her laugh at him and then listen as he threatened her. It all played out in silence, but then she picked up the drink. I had been watching the drink, focusing on it as much as I could. Thankfully, his phone didn't swing around quite as much as Kristina's did, so I had been able to track the position of the drink on and off for about sixty seconds before Kristina picked it up. Going back, we could see that Melanie had definitely picked up the same glass, taken a sip and put it back down. It happened between Kristina laughing and Paul threatening her, and he had clearly handed his phone to someone else at that point because he moved into the shot with his back to the camera. Which was the problem because he completely blocked our view of the glass.

'I couldn't see what happened between Melanie putting it down and Kristina picking it up,' said Barbie. 'There were so many people milling about behind them and around them that it was impossible to track them all. I could see Michael again, but I still couldn't see what he had in his hands and this time it looked like he never reached Kristina. He was getting close before she picked up the drink, but he hadn't reached her.'

I thought for a second. 'There were two glasses.'

'Hmmm?'

'Take the footage back. There were two glasses.' Barbie did as I requested, scrolling back through the film to a point when the counter was in shot. There were indeed two glasses that looked exactly the same. Both had a half orange, half red look to them that screamed cocktail. I believed it was called a sweet sunrise, but I couldn't name the ingredients. 'Take it back further,' I insisted. 'I want to see how the drinks get there.'

Wordlessly, Barbie complied, winding back the film until we accepted that what we were seeing didn't show it. 'I'll switch to Kristina's film,' said Barbie as she shut down what she was looking at and opened a different file. Once again, we stared at the tiny screen as the drama played out.

'There!' we both yelled together.

'Um, are you guys okay in there?' asked a man's voice from outside the bathroom door. 'It's cool to sneak off for sex and all, but some of us really need to pee now.'

We exchanged a glance that admitted we had probably been in here longer than was decent or even fair to others but on the screen held in Barbie's hand was a shot of Melanie carrying both drinks.

She had brought the poison to Kristina after all.

Misdirection

Further thumping on the door broke our concentration. 'Come on guys, or I'm going to wet myself,' the voice outside insisted.

'Um, how do you want to do this?' asked Barbie in a hushed voice.

I wasn't of a mind for further subterfuge, so I went to the door and unlocked it, winked at the man desperate to get in and as he passed me, I nodded toward Barbie and said, 'Your turn.' The ambiguous statement caught him off guard, making him flick his gaze between Barbie and me until he decided his bladder was just too full to contemplate anything other than getting it emptied. The sound of him peeing filled the air before Barbie could escape and shut the door behind her.

'Really, Patty, you are naughty sometimes,' Barbie chided as we stole away, leaving the man to relieve himself. Then she sighed. 'Patty, do you really think she might have done it?'

'No, Barbie, I think everyone has the whole thing wrong.'

'How so?'

'I don't think Kristina was the intended victim. I think whoever poisoned that drink was trying to kill Melanie.'

Barbie gasped, 'Oh, my God, Why?'

'I'm not certain. But I do intend to find out.' Then I said, 'Follow me on this and see if it makes sense to you, okay?' When she nodded, I started laying out my theory. 'We saw Melanie drink out of the same glass as Kristina but the cyanide had no effect on her so it couldn't have been in the drink when she brought it across the room. We know they both drank from it because two shades of lipstick were found on the broken glass. We also know the barmen were using shaved ice in their drinks not ice cubes, but Kristina's drink had ice cubes in it, so the poison was introduced after Melanie had drunk from it and put it down. Melanie couldn't have brought ice cubes with her, nor could anyone else; it's just too hot. Anyone arriving with them would have to have brought a cooler of some kind. Also, I don't think the person administering the poison would want to touch it, so they probably had on a prophylactic glove and there was a faint handprint made from the powder you get inside the gloves left on Kristina's top. So, whoever put the ice cubes in Melanie's drink then touched Kristina. Furthermore, we have to consider that Michael somehow ingested or otherwise got poisoned but only with a small amount.'

'Yes, but surely if he was the killer, he must have touched it. Perhaps he got some on his fingers and absentmindedly touched them to his mouth,' she posited.

'That is a possibility,' I conceded. 'But what if the cyanide was planted on him? What if he was lured here because the killer knew his presence would create a distraction? If we assume that Melanie was the intended victim and the poison was in her drink that Kristina picked up by mistake, then Michael could have ingested a tiny amount of the poison from the drink that Melanie poured over his head. Do you remember who gave her the drink?'

I checked Barbie's face to see if she had kept up with me or thought I was failing to make sense. She was on the same track as me though, the clues were pointing to one person: Kristina's father. 'Why would he do it though. It makes no sense,' she said.

'That's the bit I haven't worked out,' I admitted. 'What would motivate her father to kill her?'

'He's not her father!' blurted Barbie. 'I hadn't realised you didn't know. He's, like, her mum's fourth husband. I never met him before today. Growing up, there was a totally different man living here and he was her third husband. I think Kristina came from a one-night thing on the road when she was a singer.'

'Oh, my God. That makes perfect sense.' Then my face flushed as a clue I hadn't realised was a clue raised a flag in my head to get my attention. 'Wait a second. I heard her call him daddy.'

Barbie and I both stared at each other for a heartbeat, then in unison we screeched, 'They were sleeping together!'

The conclusion we reached simultaneously made sense but there were still unanswered questions. Barbie asked the most obvious one, 'So, where did the money in Melanie's purse come from?'

I had already thought about that. I had been thinking about it for the last half hour, in fact, and now I knew the answer. 'I think Melanie found out about the relationship. She worked closely with Kristina, maybe they even talked about it. Do you think Melanie would blackmail him?'

Perplexed by the concept, Barbie said, 'I want to say no, Patty. It would explain everything though.'

I started moving toward the door. 'We have to find him. I'm going to call Jermaine.' I pulled my phone from my bag, scrolled and hit dial. It rang and then came up busy. I tried again with the same result, this time I accepted that he was rejecting the call, probably because he was being quiet somewhere.

Barbie had been looking over my shoulder. 'What do we do now?' she asked.

'We go looking for Mary Blue's husband. If he… hold on, do you know his name? I keep referring to him as he.'

'Um, no,' Barbie replied. 'I never met him before today.'

'Hmm, well then, if he is a killer, I just sent Jermaine off by himself to find him. He will have no idea he is walking into danger. We need to find him right now.' With a determined pace, I set off back to the orangery and the cops I hoped to find there. I had to get access to the rest of the house so we could find him.

The number of people in the room had reduced again, but I ignored all of them and went to the door leading back to the house. The cop there held up his hand to stop us. He was somewhere around thirty and going soft about his middle, a doughy-looking roll visibly sitting on top of his belt. 'You need to stay here until you have been cleared to go, ladies.' His tone betrayed that he had already delivered the same message plenty of times in the last hour. 'There are refreshments and bathrooms here. We won't keep you much longer.'

'Officer, the detectives have the wrong person in custody, the real killer is somewhere in this house and our friend went to find him more than an hour ago.'

The cop just stared at me, bored. When he finally he spoke, he said, 'Sorry, I was waiting for the punchline. No one gets to leave no matter how kooky their story.'

I turned to Barbie. 'Your turn.'

Caught by surprise, she said, 'Oh, err, yes okay.' Then she stepped into the space I stepped out of and flashed him her wonderful smile.

He glanced at her impressive chest, looked back up and said, 'Don't even bother, sugar. My wife has a pair just like that at home.'

'Just like that?' I asked, doubtful that any part of his wife looked anything like any part of Barbie.

He tilted his head, acknowledging that I had a point, but said, 'No one gets to leave until they have given their details and we are satisfied that they are no longer needed.'

He didn't look likely to budge, but as I looked about desperately for the cop that looked most likely to deal with us next, I heard a door open and the annoying voice of detective Davis reached my ears.

'Detective Davis,' I called out loudly. 'Detective Davis, I have evidence for you.' I fell silent again, listening to see if he had heard me and moved right up to where pudgy cop was blocking the door. When the detective came into view at the end of the corridor, we saw that Melanie was right behind him, her hands in cuffs behind her back and being walked along by a uniformed cop. Bringing up the rear was Detective Sergeant Washington.

'What is it this time?' asked the young detective, though it was clear he had no interest in listening. 'Did you find Jimmy Hoffa's last resting place? Have you solved the mystery of the Big Foot?' The pudgy cop next to me sniggered.

'Let the lady speak, Ben.' His elder colleague was frowning in response to his young colleague's ridiculous response.

'You hang around and listen to her nonsense if you want, Mike,' he snapped. 'I have my suspect. We are going downtown so she can have a lawyer waste a load of time trying to wiggle her out of the murder she committed with her boyfriend. If he survives, maybe they can hold hands as they get the lethal injection.' Then, the awful man started moving again, yelling impatiently for the uniformed man to keep up.

Just as Melanie was about to vanish from view, I yelled, 'Melanie, were you blackmailing Mary's husband?'

Her eyes went wide in surprise just as the cop nudged her forward and she was lost to sight.

Detective sergeant Washington didn't follow them though. He was looking at me with his arms crossed in front of his chest. He had the look of a man that believed he might have missed something or hadn't taken everything into consideration. I watched him come to a decision and start down the corridor toward us. 'What is it that you think that you know, Mrs...'

'Fisher,' I supplied. 'Patricia Fisher.'

Barbie piped up, 'Patty is a real gumshoe. She solves mysteries all the time.' She delivered the statement with her usual exuberance, all but bouncing in her excitement.

'Is that so?' said Detective Sergeant Washington. 'I can't say the same. The cases we get hardly ever get solved. This one looks almost like an open and shut case though. So easy to solve, in fact, that it is making me suspicious. So, tell me what we missed.'

He was acting as if I was going to hurt his feelings or make him feel inadequate if I had worked it out when he hadn't, but I wasn't going to let concern for his feelings slow me down. I tried to push my way by the pudgy cop again so I could join the detective, but he put his arm out to bar my way. 'No one leaves until they are released,' he reminded me, this time sounding impatient.

'Don't be such an idiot, man,' said the detective with a sigh, then he beckoned for Barbie and me to join him.

The cop's arm dropped though his expression was livid. I paid him no attention, focusing on the detective as I said, 'Can we talk on the way? I am concerned about my friend.'

'I'm calling him again now,' said Barbie with her phone to an ear.

'What friend?' the detective asked, sounding confused, as I and then Barbie dashed by him to get to the stairs.

The Husband

'We have been looking at the live-feed footage that was taken at the party immediately before and after Kristina was poisoned,' I started to explain as we went up the stairs.

Sergeant Washington interrupted me, 'I have already seen it. It shows the suspect taking the drink to the victim. It is the single most damning piece of evidence.' After he spoke, he fell silent again, waiting for me to say something more and possibly hoping that he hadn't already disproved the theory I was about to reveal.

We had reached the wrap-around upstairs landing and paused. 'It showed that she had two drinks. One for her and one for Kristina, but it also showed her drinking from the same glass immediately before Kristina picked it up. I believe Kristina was never the intended target. There were ice cubes in the glass which I believe was the method the killer used to get the poison into her drink.' I had his attention. 'Melanie picks the glass up, takes a drink and puts it down, so the killer, who is watching from somewhere behind her, marks it as her glass and drops in the ice cubes when no one is looking. The killer gets lucky because even though he has arranged a distraction through the manipulation of an unwitting accomplice in the form of Michael Torrence, Paul Rodriguez gets into it with Kristina and all eyes are on them. However, what he cannot predict is that Kristina will pick up the wrong glass.'

'Okay,' said Detective Sergeant Washington. 'Let's assume I believe you. How do you explain the money in her purse?'

I smiled as I replied, 'I'm glad you asked. The answer ties into the reason Melanie, and not Kristina, was the target. Melanie discovered that Kristina was sleeping with her mother's husband. I believe she was blackmailing him. The money you found was him paying for her silence, but he had already decided it would be simpler to kill her, so he arranged for her ex-boyfriend to come to the party. Probably telling him that he would put in a good word. He knew Kristina would react to his presence and intended to use that as a distraction. He brought the two girls drinks already, and put cyanide in the one he handed Melanie, but she dumped it over Michael Torrence's head which is how he came to ingest a non-lethal dose.'

Sergeant Washington was frowning as he considered all that I had just said. 'Do you have any evidence, Mrs Fisher?' the ageing detective asked.

'Not one bit,' I confessed. 'But, if we find the man, we find the evidence. He is in this house somewhere. I sent my butler, Jermaine, to find him almost ninety minutes ago because I wanted to check he wasn't going to harm himself and because I knew he had been standing close to Kristina when she died and might have seen something. However, I haven't heard from Jermaine in a while and he isn't answering his phone.' I looked at Barbie who just shook her head and slipped her phone away again; she couldn't raise him.

'The ice cubes had to come from a freezer on the premises so the subset of people with access to them, if we ignore staff, is very few.'

'You don't know that the poison was in the ice cubes,' he countered.

'No, I don't. But I do know that no one else had ice cubes in their drink. No one,' I repeated for emphasis.

Detective Sergeant Washington inclined his head. 'Okay. I'll go with it. So, what was Michael Torrence doing with cyanide pills in his pocket?' he asked.

It was the perfect question. 'He was the patsy. The killer knew that Michael and Kristina had beef and that he would create a scene if he came here. We even watched Mary Blue's husband tackle him to the ground; the perfect opportunity to slip the evidence into the man's jacket.'

The grey-haired detective nodded his head slowly. Considering everything I had told him, he scratched his head and pulled a face, but said, 'Oh, what the hell, I've followed worse leads and I'm already here. Let's see if we can find Mr Blake.'

'Who's Mr Blake?' I asked. 'Is that the name of Mary Blue Wilshaw's husband?'

'It is,' he replied simply. 'Francis Blake, a former Major League baseball star. You haven't heard of him?

'I'm British,' I said, believing that was sufficient explanation.

'Yeah, okay,' he conceded. 'Well, I guess he was good-looking enough to attract Mrs Wilshaw, but he was penniless. He quite famously started his own tech firm called Offspring Vitality. Have you heard of them? He was something of a rival for Apple for a while but there was a fatal flaw in his software, and it all died in the millennium bug.'

'Oh, yeah, I heard about that. Didn't the problem wipe out several Wall Street firms?' I still didn't recognise his name, but I remembered the firm and the scandal.

'That's right,' confirmed the older man. 'He got sued by every customer he ever sold to and had to file for bankruptcy. Shall we have a look for him?'

For the next ten minutes we went room to room. It was my guess that he was upstairs because there were so many people downstairs. He would find it hard to move without running into a cop on the lower floor.

He would have tucked himself away in a bedroom somewhere, playing the part of grieving father-figure and undoubtedly told any cops that spoke to him that he had no idea why anyone would want Kristina dead. He would be panicking though. Melanie was alive and if I was right about the sex and the blackmail, she was going to put two and two together soon.

As I thought that, I blurted out the answer to his whereabouts, 'He'll be in the garage!' We had exhausted almost all the rooms upstairs, but the garage is where we should have started looking.

Detective sergeant Washington looked sceptical. 'We should check all the rooms up here first. There are some left at the end here we haven't looked in.'

Ignoring him, I grabbed Barbie's hand and we were running, leaving the older man behind as I raced to search where I was convinced Kristina's killer would be. He must have been feeling the noose tighten and would have wanted to escape before Melanie cracked under interview and admitted the affair and the blackmail. He couldn't know how much time he had, so would be in the garage waiting to escape as soon as the cops cleared out.

Barbie knew where she was going, telling me how it used to be a great place to sneak off as teenagers when Kristina swiped booze from her mother's cabinet. We accessed it through a door in the kitchen, and there, caught like a criminal in a search beam, was Francis Blake. He had his hands on the raised tailgate of a BMW X6. It made a quiet beep and started to lower as Barbie and I walked into the garage, the clip-clopping of our heels echoing in the large open space.

'Where are you going, Francis?' I asked.

He walked around to the driver's door. 'What business is that of yours?' he asked in an unfriendly tone.

Where the heck was Jermaine?

Francis opened his car door and leaned in, pressing a button inside I guess because the roller door in front of the car began to open. He was about to get in when I blurted, 'I know it was you!'

He had one leg inside the car and a hand on the handle above his head so he could swing in and up onto the seat. My shout made him pause. 'I have no idea what you are talking about,' he replied, turning his head in my direction to deliver the lie.

'You put the cyanide in the ice cube, didn't you?' My voice echoed in the open space of the room. He didn't reply but he did stop to listen. I pressed on. 'There's only a few people that could have done it; the ice would have melted in the heat, so they had to be fresh from a freezer in the house. You wore a glove to keep the cyanide from your hand but when you saw Kristina fall you raced to her side and touched her. You had just slipped the glove off, but your hand left a trace of the powder on her clothing. Melanie found out about you, didn't she? She knew you were sleeping with Kristina and was blackmailing you. But you knew about Kristina interfering in her relationship with Michael so you invited him here because you knew he would cause a distraction. That was your chance, wasn't it? But you couldn't predict that Kristina would pick up Melanie's drink and you had distanced yourself, so you didn't even see her do it.'

Through gritted teeth, he said, 'None of that matters anymore. I'm leaving now and there's nothing you can do to stop me.'

The roller door was still winding up toward the ceiling, but Barbie saw an opportunity and acted. While Francis hesitated, she grabbed a toolchest on wheels, manoeuvring it in front of his car to block his path.

He laughed at her efforts, 'What's that supposed to do? I can just nudge it out of the way with my car.' He flipped his eyebrows at me, as if he was winking, then slid into the car and shut the door. Barbie though, wasn't finished. She reached down, squatting low to grip beneath the heavy chest of tools which she then tipped over. As she stood back up, her face flushed from exertion, I caught a triumphant smile as it played across her lips. She might be petite but countless hours in the gym had also made her strong.

The car door burst open again and this time the expression Francis bore was easy to read; he was mad. He was also armed, a small automatic handgun appearing in his right hand as he levelled it at my head. My bladder threatened to betray me, and my feet wouldn't move; I hate guns. 'So, you think you have me caught, do you?' he raged.

'LAPD! Drop your weapon!' the shout came from behind me and to my left where the door led into the garage from the house. Detective Sergeant Washington had found us. My mouth had gone dry in terror, but I could see the indecision in Francis's face. His gun was still pointing at me, but he would never get the shot off. If his trigger finger twitched, Detective Sergeant Washington would shoot him, and the distances were such that he couldn't miss.

Francis knew it too, the decision to live and go to jail for his crime rather than die now resulted in his whole body wilting as his right arm lowered. He hung his head to stare at the concrete floor as the detective began moving forward to take him into custody. Before he got to him, Francis looked up again, misery etched on his face, 'I loved Kristina. I really did. I didn't mean to pois...'

The boom that echoed in the garage startled me, deafened me and seemed to reach inside me to rattle my bones. Directly in front of me, Francis looked down at the growing red patch on his white polo shirt. He looked back up at me, opened his mouth to say something, then seemed to fold into himself as he slumped to the floor.

'LAPD! Drop your weapon!' shouted Detective Sergeant Washington again. Somewhere in my brain I had already known that the shot hadn't come from him. He was to my left; the shot had come from the right. Detective Sergeant Washington was moving, crossing the room behind me. I turned to see who had shot Francis and there was Mary Blue Wilshaw, her right hand still holding the gun as a wisp of smoke escaped the barrel.

'Perhaps I should take that, madam,' said Jermaine, coming alongside Mary Blue to pluck the weapon from her grasp. There was an ugly lump on the left side of his forehead and a trickle of blood running from it where the skin had split.

As Kristina's mum was taken into custody and the cops fruitlessly gave emergency treatment to her husband, Barbie and I were taken to stand at the edge of the garage by detective sergeant Washington. Barbie was holding my hand, but I think it was for her comfort rather than mine.

Jermaine assured us that his head was fine but did not resist when a handsome young black male cop came to check the wound anyway. The coroner in the cheap suit was having a busy day, confirming death at the scene for Francis after finishing with Kristina and the same CSI guys were now looking for the ejected bullet case not far from where Barbie and I were standing. Once Detective Sergeant Washington had taken Mary Blue Wilshaw into custody, other cops had rushed into the room with their guns raised, drawn to the scene by the sound of the fatal gunshot. The garage had been very exciting for a few seconds until they realised Barbie and I posed no threat. Now we were waiting just outside the garage while the law enforcement professionals went about their tasks.

'This is all so terrible,' murmured Barbie. She wasn't in shock, but I could tell she was rattled by the recent events. When we left the ship a few hours ago, she was filled with excitement at the prospect of seeing her friends. Now I could only imagine she wished she had been pressed into working on board today instead.

I saw Detective Sergeant Washington approaching. He was coming out of the garage and toward the light, the change in brightness causing him to squint. He said, 'I spoke with Detective Davis. Your friend will be released shortly. All charges have been dropped. Can I arrange for you to be taken somewhere?' he asked.

'We have a driver, thank you though. Are we free to go?' I asked. I hadn't called the driver yet because I didn't know when we would be released but I hoped he wasn't too far away; I was ready to leave.

'You will both need to give statements,' the detective replied.

Barbie had a question. 'Will there be any need for us to return for a trial?' she asked.

The detective considered that for a moment. 'You're on a cruise ship, right?'

'Yes,' she replied. 'I work on board, but Patty is a guest and Jermaine is her butler.'

'Butler?' Now he was giving me a quizzical look, probably wondering why I didn't look or sound like a person with a travel-along butler.

'It's a long story,' I replied with a shrug.

'Well, to answer your question; I will have to check, but I don't think so. You were not witness to anything that I did not see. The case against Mrs Wilshaw is very simple and there will be no case against Mr Blake because he is dead. If you were suspects, there would be cause to deny your release, but you are not, so I believe your statements will be sufficient.'

In all it was a further forty-five minutes before we were released during which time Jermaine told the cops about how he had followed Mr Blake and become suspicious because the man was clearly packing. Then, peeking around a doorframe, he saw him take an ice cube tray out of a freezer in an upstairs pantry but lost sight of him again. Jermaine tried to catch up, but Mr Blake had been waiting for him and hit him with a golf club. Several of the cops had winced at that point and stared at the egg-shaped lump on Jermaine's forehead.

The ice cube tray was found in Francis's luggage in the boot of his car and with our statements taken and our driver waiting, there was nothing left to do.

As we slipped into the air-conditioned luxury of the limousine for the hour-long ride back to the Aurelia, I considered asking if anyone wanted a cocktail from the bar in the back of the car. But dismissed the notion, closed my eyes and went to sleep on Jermaine's shoulder.

The End

Except it really isn't, there's an entire series waiting for you to discover and it doesn't end there because there are 30 books planned and a second series picks up as soon as this one finishes. Now on to the next short story, which develops a character introduced in one of Patricia's books.

Albert and his dog, Rex Harrison, have marvellous adventures when they decide to take a culinary tour of Great Britain. Albert is a retired detective superintendent and Rex was a police dog until he got fired for having a bad attitude. As you might imagine, they get into all manner of scrapes on their trip. This short story occurs a short while before they set off.

Hellcat

Albert Smith's Culinary Capers

Short Story

Steve Higgs

Table of Contents

More Books by Steve Higgs

Free Books and More

Missing Rings

Albert frowned, his face creasing as he began poking about. Petunia's collection of engagement, wedding, and eternity rings were not where they always sat on her dressing table. They were there yesterday, weren't they? How could they go missing?

Rex wandered into his human's bedroom, wagging his tail lazily from side to side until he caught the scent of the cat. The unwelcome scent meant the cat had been in here again. He'd caught it sitting on his human's bed just yesterday, but this wasn't the lingering smell from then, this was fresh. He jumped up to put his front paws on the bed, sniffing along the cover to find the spot it had occupied.

'Down, Rex,' commanded his human, a kindly old man whose nose was just as unused as all others of his species. So far as Rex was concerned, humans were fun to be around, but also intensely frustrating as they ran around using their eyes and ears, when the information was right there if they would just sniff it in.

Albert stared at the dressing table again, moving things around until he spotted the glint of gold. There they were, he signed with relief. His eldest grandson was planning to propose, he discovered yesterday. Martin was twenty-seven, a sensible age to be tying the knot, and though he hadn't been asked, Albert wanted to offer the ring he bought Petunia when he asked for her hand. It was a two-carat diamond with a cluster of lesser diamonds around it. It cost a silly amount at the time; three months wages, if his memory served him correctly, but she had been worth every hard-earned penny.

His frown returned: the engagement ring wasn't there. The eternity and wedding band were, but not the one he wanted. How had they come to move anyway? Turning to spy the dog, an oversized German Shepherd, who was now lifting the valance with his head as he looked under the bed, Albert said, 'Rex!' to get the dog's attention. He raised his voice to see if he could make the dog jump and chuckled when he heard the animal knock his head against the underside of the bed.

Rex popped back out, a scowl on his face. He played tricks on his human regularly - looking under things until his human gave in and got on the carpet to see what he was looking at was a favourite. He fell for it every time, even though there was never anything there to look at. However, it simply wasn't on for his human to get his own back.

'Rex, have you been in here messing with things?' asked Albert.

Rex raised one eyebrow. 'It was the cat. Can you seriously not smell it? It smells like evil mixed with gone-off fish.'

Albert stared down at the dog, wondering what the odd whining/chuffing noises were all about. 'Honestly, dog, I swear you are trying to answer me sometimes.'

Rex walked up to the dressing table and gave it a sniff. Then made a surprised face because there was visible cat fur among the items displayed. Looking up at his human, Rex would have shaken his head if he knew to do so.

A knock at the door disturbed them and Rex exploded into action. He loved when people came to the door. It was the unexpected element that triggered his excitement. Behind the door could be anyone! It could be the postman with a parcel, or one of his human's children with his or her family; that was always fun. Or, it might be someone calling to see if Albert wanted to go to the pub. That happened sometimes. Forgetting the cat for a moment, Rex barked and ran, charging down the stairs to run at the door where he leapt up to place his front paws either side of the small frosted-glass window. A whiff of Old Spice cologne and moustache wax told him the person outside was the man from across the street.

Albert put the two rings into his trouser pocket as he made his way down to the front door. He had to fight Rex to get him out of the way, eventually shoving the daft dog back and holding his collar with one hand so he could open the door. The shadow outside proved to be Wing Commander Roy Hope, Albert's neighbour from across the road.

Albert wasn't expecting him, but the two men got on well and saw each other in church each week. Their wives had gone to school together and were friends their whole lives. Albert's wife, Petunia, had been gone for most of a year now, and the couple across the street liked to check in on him semi-regularly. Albert greeted his caller. 'Good morning, Roy.'

Roy wasn't one for chit chat, especially not when he had a purpose. 'I say, old boy, you've got a snooper.'

'A what?' said Albert, not sure he'd heard correctly.

'A snooper,' announced Roy again, speaking loudly as was his habit. However, he then leaned in close to whisper surreptitiously, 'It's that woman from number twenty-three. The odd-looking one who just moved in. She's up to something,' he concluded confidently.

Albert, a seventy-eight-year-old retired detective superintendent, was known by his children for poking his nose in when he thought a crime might be occurring, but he hadn't noticed anything untoward about the new neighbour two doors down. 'When you say snooping...' Albert prompted Roy for more.

Roy wriggled his upper lip, an act which made his pure-white bushy moustache dance about. 'She was looking through your windows, old boy. I saw her, blatant and bold as brass. Cupped her hands either side of her head and looked through your windows. Then she moved to a different spot. 'I dare say she was casing the joint and getting ready to burgle you.'

Albert almost snorted a laugh. The lady in question was in her mid-twenties and chose to dress in a manner which residents of the village might think unusual or odd, as Roy chose to put it. She was an EMO, Albert thought, though he struggled to keep up with all the fashions and trends now. Her clothing was mostly black and had a ravaged look to it. Apparently, it could be bought like that, even though, to Albert's mind, the wearer looked to have lost a fight with a tiger. The laugh which started to form, died when he remembered his wife's missing engagement ring. 'When was this?' he asked.

'Yesterday, old boy. And again this morning.'

Albert's eyebrows made a bid for freedom, hiking up his forehead as they tried to reach the summit of his scalp. Leaning from his door and craning his neck around to look in the direction of her house, he said, 'You say she was looking through my windows?' The comment was made more to himself than to Roy. 'I think I might need to find out who she is.'

Rex had been waiting patiently, but the scent of the cat was ripe on the air. Trained by the police to discern different smells, he'd qualified as a police dog only to be fired months later for having a bad attitude. The only dog in the history of the Metropolitan Police to ever get the sack, Rex had been loyal and obedient to his human handlers but despairing of their inability to use their olfactory systems to smell the clues. He generally worked out who the killer/robber/criminal was within minutes and got upset when the humans wouldn't listen to him.

The cat had been in his house, and Rex was going to have a word with it.

'Rex!' shouted Albert as his dog ran across the front lawn and leapt the low hedge into his neighbour's garden.

'Won't be a minute!' barked Rex.

'What's got him so excited?' asked Roy.

Albert muttered some expletives, ducking back into his house to snag the dog lead from its hook. Then, when Rex stopped at number twenty-three and started sniffing around the house, he saw an opportunity.

'It would appear that I need to retrieve my dog,' he announced as if orating to the back row of a theatre. He'd spotted something of interest already and had a legitimate reason to take a closer look.

'You're going over there, old boy?' Roy wiggled his moustache, and set off too, ambling down the street with a sense of righteous purpose.

Rex would go into the house to find the cat if someone would open the door, but he could smell that the cat had been through the overgrown undergrowth at the front of the house in the last few minutes. That meant it might still be outside. He followed the smell to the side of the house where a tall wrought iron gate barred his progress.

He could hear his human calling his name. A quick glance over his shoulder revealed the old man and his friend with the facial hair coming to him. Heaven's be praised, they understood for once: the cat needed to be taught a lesson.

He pawed the gate, making it clang as it moved, but it wouldn't open. Frustrated, Rex peered into the dark space down the side of the house where the gate led to a path overgrown with more weeds and shaded by an out-of-control wisteria. The scent of the cat was rife now, though Rex couldn't believe it when the evil feline wandered into view.

Rex barked his displeasure. The cat sat on its haunches and began to lazily lick a front paw. This was the first time Rex had seen it. Until now, all he got was the smell to let him know it had been in his garden and into his house, finding itself a comfortable place to sleep on his human's bed – a place where Rex wasn't allowed to go! The cat was missing its left eye, which gave it a hellish appearance when combined with the tattered left ear. Then Rex noticed the stumpy tail when the cat flicked it in an annoyed way.

Rex barked again, louder this time, letting the cat know what was in store if Rex caught it on his land again. The cat flicked its tail and sauntered away in an overly casual manner.

Albert and Roy arrived at the front of the property, opening the garden gate to proceed down the path to the door.

Seeing them, Rex barked, crouching his front end, and signalling as the police handlers had taught him. 'It's right down here! Open the gate and I'll get it!' Rex knocked the gate again with his skull, keen to get through it and teach the cat a swift lesson in humility.

From his front door, Albert could see an envelope dangling from the letterbox. Rex's decision to go to the property gave him a perfect reason to see if the homeowner's name was on it.

'Why is he barking madly like that?' asked Roy. He couldn't see anything that would make the dog want to continue to bark.

Roy's question gave Albert pause, his dismissive answer about the dog being bonkers dying on his lips as he observed Rex's behaviour. Was he alerting? That's what it looked like. He knew Rex's background as a police dog. Albert's three children were all serving senior police officers; a call to his youngest one was all it took to scoop one of many dogs who failed the training. He only found out afterwards that he'd been duped and given a problem dog who passed the training but then couldn't be managed.

Whatever the case, Rex was displaying behaviour he'd seen before in other police dogs. If he were interpreting it correctly, his dog could smell one of three things: drugs, guns, or cash. 'Rex, to me,' he used his insistent voice and the dog complied.

'It's back there somewhere,' Rex whined. 'I'm not going to hurt it. I just want to make sure it doesn't come into the house again.'

To Roy, Albert murmured, 'I need to make a phone call.'

Professional Busybody

Albert stayed in his neighbour's front garden confident his dog had made so much noise that there couldn't be anyone home. Yet if someone did come to the door, Albert had a line prepared in his head about wanting to welcome their new neighbour in person. He plucked the envelope from the letterbox, fishing for his reading glasses only to discover he'd left them at home

Albert offered the letter to Roy with his left hand, using his right to dig around for his phone. 'Can you read this and tell me what name is on the address?'

Thinking it likely the letter was for the previous resident since the new owner only just moved in, Albert was pleased when Roy said, 'Ophelia James.' The person in the house previously was Darren somethingorother.

The ringing in his ear stopped when his call was answered, the voice of his youngest son echoing loud and clear. 'Hello, Dad.'

'Are you at work?' Albert asked, getting straight to the point – a trait he'd instilled in his children at an early age.

At the other end of the call, Chief Inspector Randall Smith pursed his lips. His dad didn't call very often, and when he did, it tended to be because he wanted to know something he couldn't find out for himself. 'I am,' Randall replied cautiously.

'Super.' Albert grinned at Roy and waggled his eyebrows. 'Can you look up the name Ophelia James for me, please, son?'

Randall sighed. As he suspected, his father was poking his nose into someone's business. It wasn't the first time, it wouldn't be the last, but helping him with information generally resulted in trouble. 'I don't think I should do that, dad.'

Albert's smile froze. 'Why ever not? I think I'm onto something, Randall.'

'Like the time you thought the verger was sending poison pen letters?' Randall reminded him.

'He *was* sending them!' snapped Albert. 'He got arrested for it last week.'

This was news to Randall, not that he expected to hear of every crime committed in his home county; he worked in London after all. Nevertheless, he narrowed his eyes and questioned his father. 'Are you making that up, dad?'

'No! Patricia Fisher caught him. She's got quite the nose for solving crime, that one. She should have gone into the police herself.'

Dismissing that line of conversation, Randall said, 'Who is Ophelia James and what is it that you think she might have done?'

Albert thought about how to answer Randall's question in such a way that his son would relent and use his computer to provide the information he wanted. He couldn't think of anything though, so he just said, 'She's been looking through my windows and your mother's engagement ring is missing. Also, Rex is alerting at her house so there might be drugs here. Or a body,' Albert added quickly, thinking it might prompt his son to comply. 'There's definitely something going on and I just want you to check to see if she has a record.'

'I'm sorry, Dad. I have an insurance scam case I need to crack. All my time has to be devoted to that.'

'Insurance scam you say?' Albert feigned interest, hoping to keep his son talking long enough to change his mind.

Randall groaned. 'Yes, Dad. A person gets a call from a firm who sound real, has a website, and are offering a great introductory rate. They target older people a lot; it's all very ugly and they can get away with people's life savings. Anyway, there's a new crew operating in this area and I'm getting a lot of pressure to catch them. If you don't mind, Dad. I really need to get back to the investigation I am supposed to be leading.'

Albert could sense that further persistence would lead to an argument and he remembered being under pressure to produce a result. To end the call, he said, 'Very good, Randall. I'm sure you'll get them.'

Roy, who hadn't heard the other half of the conversation, asked, 'We are on our own?'

'Very much,' Albert grumbled. Skewing his lips to one side, he fished the rings from his pocket to show Roy. 'My Petunia's engagement ring is missing. Quite inexplicably missing,' he added. 'It was there the last time I looked, which might have been yesterday, but someone had disturbed the things on her dressing table, and they took her diamond engagement ring. I was planning to give it to my grandson if he wanted it.'

Roy narrowed his eyes at Mrs James's front door. 'And this woman has been snooping at your windows, old boy. I dare say there's a connection.'

Rex listened to the exchange, pointing out each time either human paused that it was the cat they needed to speak to. They just weren't listening, a human trait which had always irked him. The cat was here somewhere, possibly inside the house if the back door was open or it had one of those cat flap thingies.

He chose to investigate again since the humans were just standing around talking.

Albert was faced with a dilemma. Law abiding his entire life - he had to be, of course, but his wife's ring was missing, and this woman had been looking through his windows. He reached a decision, stepping forward to rap his knuckles smartly on the doorframe.

'You going to confront her, old boy?' asked Roy, somewhat surprised by the escalation.

Albert turned his head to the side and spoke over his shoulder, 'I'm going to introduce myself and ask if there was something she wanted. I can make out like I saw her outside my house. I'll be the friendly neighbour, and we shall see how she responds. You can tell if a person is lying by what their eyes do,' he told Roy knowingly.

He didn't get to check out her eyes though because no one came to the door. He chose to try again, opting to use the heavy brass knocker on the door this time. However, when he lifted it, the door moved: it wasn't closed, only pushed to. With the slightest tap of his index finger, the door moved two inches.

Rex got no luck at the side of the house, the cat hadn't returned to taunt him from behind the gate, but when he looked back at the two humans, he saw they had the front door open. Rex had never really understood the concept of property: if he peed on it, it was his. Wasn't that a simpler solution? Humans had all manner of strange rules about who could go where. Rex chose to ignore them because they made no sense, saw the chance to get his own back on the cat by invading the cat's place which he intended to mark as his own once inside, and ran for the widening gap.

Albert never saw him coming, the dog streaking past his legs to fly inside the house. 'Rex, no!' he yelled, which had as much effect as throwing a spider web in front of a charging bull.

'I know you're in here, cat!' barked Rex. 'Let's see how you like it! Where's your favourite spot? I'll be sure to mark that one!'

His human was shouting something discouraging - he often did. Rex, however, knew it was his job to keep the cat out of his human's house and that was what he was going to do.

Dumbfounded on the doorstep, Albert grimaced at his friend the wing commander. 'I've got to go after him. Heaven knows what damage he might do. The poor woman hasn't even had a chance to settle in yet.'

'It doesn't look like she's unpacked,' observed Roy, peering through the now wide-open door at the boxes stacked against the walls.

From inside, they could hear Rex barking. Then a thump as the dog knocked something over. Albert swore and went into the house. He knew that by law he wasn't technically breaking and entering. He didn't have the homeowner's permission, but the door was unlocked, and he would be able to argue that he felt it necessary to retrieve his dog. Another crashing noise propelled him across the threshold just in time to hear the squeal of a cat as it screeched somewhere deeper in the house.

'Should we be in here, old boy?' asked Roy, joining Albert inside the house.

Rex was barking insanely now, toward the back of the house and loud enough to alert people in the next village. The cat was spitting and hissing in return with just as much volume. Albert expected to find the cat backed into a space too small for his dumb, oversized German Shepherd to penetrate, but he didn't get the chance to find out because the next thump was followed instantly by the sound of scrambling feet as the cat ran and the dog chased.

Albert and Roy were in the narrow hallway that ran alongside the stairs when the cat rounded the corner ahead of them, leaning into the bend and running for all it was worth. It's much lower centre of gravity ensured it could turn quicker than the dog, which appeared about a heartbeat later, slamming into the wall opposite the room he was leaving because he was moving altogether too fast to change direction.

Rex struck the wood panelling with a jarring blow to his right shoulder, but it wasn't going to slow him down for long. The cat had said several unkind things about his mother and the local stray dogs – it was not the sort of thing he could forgive, not on top of the blatant home invasion. The cat had earned itself a chewed tail at the very least.

Bouncing off the wall, Rex put his head down and powered on. The cat was going to go out of the front door, he could see the opening ahead of him, daylight streaming in enticingly. Once the cat was out in the open, he would be able to catch him.

Albert's eyes flared as the cat shot between his feet and the dog looked set to follow. Mercifully, Rex made himself thin, squeezing against the wall to pass by his human's legs without touching them.

'Don't worry!' barked Rex. 'I'll get him when he goes outside!'

But the cat didn't go outside, he banked hard at the bottom of the stairs and flew up them. Rex's paws slipped and slid over the hallway carpet as he tried to follow. His butt slammed against the front door, banging it back against the wall as he finally got his legs under control.

'Rex!' Albert bellowed after the dog, but Rex was already powering up the stairs when Albert shouted, 'Leave the cat alone!'

Rex didn't slow down but he did hear what his human said. It mystified him. Why were they here if it wasn't to deal with the cat? He got to the landing and had a choice of directions. The house smelled of the cat; enough so that he was finding it difficult to determine which way the cat went. Huffing in frustration, he put his nose to the carpet and started sniffing his way along.

Albert called again, yelling the dog's name to no avail. 'I'd better go after him,' he grumbled, placing his hand on the banister.

Wondering what he ought to do and feeling like an unnecessary extra because he wasn't adding any value, Roy volunteered, 'I'll come with you. Many hands and all that.'

Both pensioners made their way up the stairs using the handrail to give them a bit of extra oomph, but just as they reached the landing and both turned right toward the front of the house, the cat shot out of a bedroom behind them and bolted back down the stairs.

Rex was hot on the cat's heels and, to Albert, it looked as if he'd managed to nip the cat's backend or tail because he had bits of fur stuck to his jowls.

Now sensing victory, Rex took the stairs in two bounds, his powerful legs driving him on at a pace the cat couldn't match. The cat's only chance was to climb, but there were no trees outside. Rex wasn't going to hurt it, he just wanted to establish some ground rules. It was bad enough that he had to share his garden with the local squirrel mafia, but a cat that believed it could come into his house and sit on his human's bed? Well, there were limits to what he would tolerate. It didn't help that the cat looked like something the devil might have vomited.

However, going as fast as possible proved to be a mistake. At the bottom of the stairs, he had altogether too much momentum to switch from a downward trajectory to a horizontal one. He crashed into the carpet, knocked into a coatrack, and slammed the door back against its stops. The cat was gone, haring across the front lawn by the time Rex looked up. Only a heartbeat had passed but the front door was swinging shut.

Snarling at his choice of pace over planning, Rex bounced back onto his feet and shot through the gap before the door slammed shut behind him with a thump.

At the top of the stairs, Albert swore yet again. The dog was finally out of the house, but the stupid beast didn't have the sense to stay where he could be found. He might chase the cat to the next county before it occurred to him to question where he was.

'Do you think we should look for Petunia's ring?' asked Roy. When Albert turned to look at him questioningly, he added, 'Since we are already here.'

It was a tempting proposition, but not a sensible one. 'We should go. The lady was snooping through my windows, that doesn't mean she came inside. It doesn't mean she did anything wrong at all. This is her house, and we shouldn't be in it.'

Roy nodded, knowing his friend was right, and they made toward the stairs.

With his foot poised to descend the first step, he heard the distinctive sound of a car pulling onto the driveway.

Trapped/Ambush

Rex leapt the fence that bordered the front of the garden, following the cat. 'I'm gonna get you, cat!' he barked as he chased after it, his tongue lolling from the right side of his mouth. He'd heard the shouts from his human - it wasn't so much that he chose to ignore him, Rex simply knew what was best. If his human's nose worked properly, he would know the cat had been in the bedroom and would be thanking Rex for his diligence.

The cat shot under a car, evading Rex just when he was almost close enough to pounce. Forced to stop and go around, Rex lost sight of the cat and had to use his nose to continue the chase. Down a side alley between the houses, Rex plunged through brambles and gnarly undergrowth that pulled at his fur. He barely noticed any of it because the cat had somehow given him the slip. Had it found a bolt hole in the mouth of the alley and slipped through it to escape?

He would have to go back and check, but he pushed on another yard first because a leafy green bush obscured what was ahead and the whole area stunk of cat. Bursting through the bush, leaves exploding in every direction, Rex skidded to a stop. It was a blind alley and he'd reached the end. He spun around to go back but, confronted with an unexpected sight, he froze to the spot in shock. Now he understood why the alleyway smelled of cats.

Back at the house, Albert and Roy were also frozen to the spot. Below them, the front door swung open - Ophelia was back from wherever she had gone, and they were intruders in her house. How could they possibly talk their way out of this one? It wasn't as if the story about the dog would work any longer, Rex was goodness knows where by now, probably still chasing the cat.

Albert felt a pang of concern for his big, dopey dog, but he had a bigger problem right now: what to do? The sensible thing would be to call out to Ophelia, give her a completely honest explanation and beg for her forgiveness. She could call the police, and if she did, he would wait patiently for their arrival. Embarrassment was the biggest issue.

Roy whispered, 'Any thoughts, old boy? We seem to have landed ourselves in a bit of a pickle.'

Unwilling to speak because he could see Ophelia from his position at the top of the stairs. She was standing in the hallway, taking off her boots, bending over awkwardly to unzip them one at a time with her left hand. Her right hand was holding her phone to her ear. Employing a professional voice, she sounded like she was selling someone a life insurance policy or something similar. Too engrossed in her work, she didn't see the two old men standing at the top of the stairs. While they gawped at her and wondered what to do, she padded out of sight through her house in stockinged feet.

If they were quick (and lucky) they might be able to slip out undetected!

'That's our gold star, award-winning policy,' Albert heard Ophelia say as he carefully placed his right foot on the next step down. 'Yes, Mrs Hatton, that will cover all your funeral expenses and leave a very worthwhile cash sum behind.' There was a pause while the person at the other end spoke; Mrs Hatton's voice impossible to hear, of course. 'Yes, we can set that up right now, Mrs Hatton. All it will take is an initial credit card payment of fifty pounds. That verifies the account and the money will be transferred to your investment pot so you're not really paying anything, you're just investing it.'

Albert listened intently for just a few seconds. He was trying to work out how to announce his presence without causing the poor woman to wet herself with fright. But as the conversation went on, he began to wonder what he was listening to. Ophelia James sounded as if she were working for a big insurance firm, but Albert had never heard of Silver Linings Life Insurance and Bond. Not that his knowledge extended to encompass every firm on the planet, but to his detective's brain, there was something fishy going on.

Roy tapped Albert on the shoulder, startling him to the point that he almost had a south of the border accident. While his heart restarted, and Roy whispered an apology, the conversation downstairs shifted gear: Mrs Hatton was ready to make her initial deposit and Ophelia was coming their way!

'Yes, Mrs Hatton. Customers who deposit over two hundred pounds when they open their account do obtain access to a higher level of interest. The ladder system Silver Linings employ has a top tier of four percent net interest for those customers able to deposit an initial sum of a thousand pounds.' She was coming back along the hall and there was nothing that way except the front door and the stairs.

Albert backed into Roy, bumping into him where he frantically gesticulated that he should turn around and start moving. 'Hide!' Albert whispered, giving his friend a shove to get him moving. There were three bedrooms and a bathroom to pick from and no way of knowing which direction might be the safe one. They turned left, toward the back of the house, their shuffling tiptoe steps carrying them swiftly into a small bedroom filled with nothing but unopened boxes.

They heard Ophelia jog up the stairs, her younger legs making a mockery of the effort it took them, but as they held their breath, uncertain where she might be heading, they heard her turn right toward the front of the house.

Peeking through a gap between the door and its frame, Albert could see her swift movements. The phone was cradled between shoulder and ear to give her two free hands. Diagonally across the corridor, he could see her frantically moving items around to uncover what she wanted: a laptop computer.

'Yes, Mrs Hatton. I can take the deposit now. You wish to take advantage of our one time only joining bonus? I must congratulate you on your vision, Mrs Hatton. You have invested wisely.' There came a brief pause while Mrs Hatton spoke, then Ophelia said, 'I just need to take the long number from your credit card.' Sixty seconds later, the call ended with a whoop as Ophelia celebrated her sale.

Albert was already more than a little suspicious, but her next words left him with no doubt.

'Another sucker,' she cheered. 'There's one born every minute.' Ophelia was scamming people, selling them a fake insurance policy, and taking their money. Her victims would never get anything for their investment and her number was most likely blocked so once the call ended their money had already been paid into her account and there was no way to get it back. There would be layers of confusion hiding the money as it transferred from one account to another, but even if the victim were to report the fraud, they willingly paid the money and who is to say what conversation had taken place after the fact.

This type of fraud was in its infancy when Albert retired from the police, and he worked murder investigations more regularly. Today he knew there were teams of boffins set up to track down criminals involved in internet and phone-based fraud. Computer forensics they called it. His kids talked about it sometimes.

The question at the front of Albert's brain now, was what to do about it?

Across the street in the alleyway between the houses, Rex found himself surrounded.

He'd run blindly into the alley, assured of his dominance and supremacy. However, the confident feeling, crashing through the undergrowth using sheer power and determination to force his way through, now seeped away as four dozen sets of eyes stared back at him.

The cat he'd been chasing stood front and centre where it meowelled at him, a deep, evil noise that spoke of violence and spitefully sharp claws. A ball of worry found its way to the pit of his stomach as yet more cats pushed their way through the undergrowth or walked along the top edge of the fence six feet above the ground.

He tried a defiant bark, 'Oh yeah, kitty cats!' Even he could hear that it sounded forced though. He backed away a pace, only to hear another cat emit its low mournful growl from the wall that blocked off the alley. Now scared for his exposed backend, Rex started to look for a way out.

The cats were edging closer, their tails bolt upright and the fur spread out to make them look like bottle brushes. Coming in on all sides and from above, there wasn't a single direction he could go that appeared to be safe.

Seeing no choice, he bunched his muscles.

Confession Time

'Randall, it's Dad,' Albert whispered into his phone.

Randall slumped his head onto his free hand. He was getting nowhere with the stupid insurance scam case and his dad wouldn't leave him alone. He accepted that he wasn't the best-behaved child growing up, but he was forty-one and surely his past crimes ought to be forgiven by now. Why was his father continuing to punish him?

'Why are you whispering, Dad?' he asked.

Albert didn't answer immediately. The sound of Ophelia moving around downstairs had stopped, like she thought she heard something and froze her body to listen more intently. When he heard her flick the kettle on, he let go the breath he held and continued to whisper, 'Son, I've got a confession to make which you won't like, but I also think I might have found your insurance scammer. Or one of them at least.'

Randall jerked forward in his chair, excited for a second, but then, analysing what his father just said, he closed his eyes to ask, 'What is the confession, Dad?'

Albert considered how to broach the subject but decided there really wasn't a good way to admit he was guilty of trespass.

'Dad?' prompted Randall, still waiting for the confession to come.

'Okay, Randall, here it is. You need to come to number twenty-three Hibiscus Drive. The woman I asked you about earlier - Ophelia James? Well she is involved in the insurance fraud you are investigating. Or she is involved in a separate insurance scam, but either way, you need to seize her laptop and have your forensic computer boffins go over it. It's in her front bedroom.'

Randall's deep frown deepened yet further, creasing his forehead to bring his hairline almost down to the point where it touched his eyebrows. 'How do you know … hold on, are you in her house?' The idea that his elderly father might misbehave that badly horrified him, but he already felt certain it was true.

'Of course not, son,' Albert lied. 'I'll explain when you get here. You probably ought to bring a crime scene van.'

Randall wanted his father's claims to be true. The computer and phone fraud people were so elusive. Catching them always took months of painstaking hard work and then they had to prove, without question, the person's criminal intentions only to find, all too often, it was the minnow they had snared, not the big fish running it. Nevertheless, he knew he had to at least check out his father's claim. He was due to brief the chief constable at five o'clock and it would be nice to have something to tell him for once.

With a huff of exhalation from his nose, Randall, pushed back his chair and started to get up. 'All right, Dad. I'll be there shortly. If you are in her house …'

'I'm not, son,' Albert lied again. Roy tugged on Albert's shirt, trying to get his attention. Albert lifted a finger to beg a moment's grace.

'Just don't be by the time I get there, okay?' warned Randall.

'We'll meet you outside.' Albert promised, hoping he could find a way to make that true. Roy was tugging on his shirt again, so he ended the call quickly by adding, 'See you soon.' Putting his phone away, he turned to see what Roy wanted so urgently and felt the blood drain from his face.

Ophelia was standing in the doorway to the back bedroom, holding a small calibre handgun on them. Cocking her head to one side, she snarled, 'Who the heck are you two?'

The cat had lured him into a blind alley and the only way out was through the platoon of feline horrors facing him. Rex leapt as the cats came for him. His powerful jaws were no match for hundreds of tiny, razor sharp claws and he knew it. His only way to minimise injury was to put his head down and run, so that was what he did.

In the house, Ophelia took a step back, leaving the doorway as she moved into the upper hallway. Her gun never wavered, pointing directly at the two men. With her left hand, she reached into the back pocket of her jeans, producing a phone. She didn't speak to Albert and Roy as she lifted it to her ear.

'Donny? Yeah, I've got intruders in my house. I think they know about the scam.' She turned her head away slightly, grimacing at whatever Donny said in reply. 'I don't know, do I? I just heard them upstairs in my house. No, the new house.' Clearly Donny was displeased with what she had to tell him. 'Look, they need to be disposed of. Just get over here.'

The call ended with a note of finality and she backed up further to the stairs. 'Come along, old codgers. You picked the wrong house to snoop today.'

'Why were you snooping at my house?' asked Albert, thinking it was a good idea to keep her talking.

Her brow furrowed. 'Your house. I have no idea who you are, old man.'

'I live at number nineteen. My name is Albert Smith and I have already called the police. They are on their way here now.'

Ophelia snorted a laugh. 'Nice try, old man. Even if the heat do show up, you won't be here and there's nothing in the house to prove I've done anything wrong. Donny's system is perfect: no overhead, isolated units working alone, undetectable. Much better than any of the other scams I've worked. Now, move!' she jerked the gun at them, beckoning they both follow.

Albert didn't want to, but he saw little option, and they couldn't hope to escape from upstairs, so they needed to go down anyway. With their hands aloft, Albert, then Roy, followed her down the stairs. Ophelia walked backwards, but the faint hope Albert held that she might trip and fall, came to naught.

Donny, it seemed, lived close by, for the call was only two minutes old when a van pulled up outside. 'You see?' smiled Ophelia, 'You'll be long gone before the police can show up. You're going for a nice drive in the countryside.'

The door opened to reveal a large man with a crew cut. He had a bullet shaped head which was tattooed to create a mask of sorts on his face and he had multiple piercings which distorted his nose, lips, and ears. His outfit, if one could even call it that, made him look like an Ewok who had been attacked with a hedge-trimmer.

Donny's face curled into an unpleasant sneer. 'Who are these two?' he growled.

Her gun still pinning both men in place, Ophelia replied, 'My neighbours, I think. That one,' she jerked the gun at Albert, 'Says I was looking through his window earlier.'

'Were you?' asked Donny.

'I was looking for my cat.'

'That flea-bitten thing is still alive?' he growled.

'You leave Hellcat alone,' she frowned. 'He and I have been through a lot together. He's just settling into a new place, that's all. He likes to explore other people's houses.'

'Yeah, whatever,' Donny shut off the conversation. 'The van's outside, and there's no one around.' He looked directly at Albert and Roy. 'I'll have to gag and tie them. I've got some carpet in the van to roll them in. They can go into Cliffe Lake. It'll be a few centuries before anyone finds them.'

Albert couldn't stop himself from gulping at the calm manner in which Donny discussed their dispatch. Behind him, Roy was fiddling with his walking cane. A nervous habit, Albert was sure.

Donny opened the front door to get the things from his van, but as he took a step forward, a blur of something brown hit his shins.

With a girlish squeal of shock, Donny flew into the air, but the blur wasn't done yet. Unable to slow down, it piled through Ophelia who was facing Albert and never even saw it coming. She too went from perpendicular to horizontal in the blink of an eye, crashing back to the hallway carpet in a confusion of limbs and a cry of pain.

Albert was fast to seize the slim chance they'd been given, kicking the gun from Ophelia's hand where it skittered free to hit the skirting board.

Roy went around Albert's back, a glint of reflected sunlight drawing Albert's eye to the thin sword the wing commander had drawn from his walking cane. His eyes went wide, but not as wide as Donny's who found the tip of the sword skewering the front of his shirt.

Like an old, yet still dashing Robin Hood, Roy barked, 'I may be getting on, young man, but I'm willing to bet my sword can find your heart before you can draw your next breath. I suggest you lie still.'

Bewildered by the turn of events, Albert looked at Rex. His dog was panting hard and he had blood dripping from half a dozen different facial cuts. With a finger pointed at Ophelia, Albert commanded, 'Rex, guard!' the dog instantly curled his top lip and growled at the woman who stank of the cat.

Outside the door, a flash of red and blue caught his attention: Randall was here, his son's disbelieving face framed in the side window of his car.

Aftermath

The sun was beginning to set when Roy's wife wandered across with his evening glass of port. She brought one for Albert too, the men clinking their small glasses together in a toast.

They were sitting on two fold-out garden chairs, also provided by Mrs Hope. Rex's wounds proved to be superficial, tiny slices in his nose, eyebrows, and ears but the combined effect made it look like he'd run though a reel of razor wire.

Randall emerged from the house, shaking his head in disbelief. 'We've got it all, Dad. The contacts on their phones have led us to the other scammers in the ring. They are all being arrested as we speak. The chief constable is over the moon.'

Donny and Ophelia had been arrested and taken away already, both protesting their innocence but with evidence stacked against them. Albert didn't think they would see freedom for a while. Her possession of a firearm and the likelihood that Donny's van had been used to transport other captive persons, would carry more weight than the fraud charges anyway.

Randall checked around to make sure no one was within earshot before lowering his voice to say, 'I just have one question, Dad. Why were you anywhere near her house?'

The sound of a cat hacking loudly stopped Albert from answering straight away, but it was his giant fearless dog backing away that made him pay attention to it. The cat was Ophelia's, they discovered. When it appeared earlier, she begged the police to look after it. They were waiting for the RSPCA to arrive because it looked like it needed urgent veterinary treatment, or perhaps euthanasia. Right now, it was hunched over, it's mouth open as it heaved a giant hairball onto the lawn.

Disgusted, but unable to look away, Albert, Roy, and Randall all saw the glint of something shiny ooze out of the slimy mess. It finally broke free of the gunk, plopping to the ground where it rolled over.

Randall moved closer, the cat opting to scurry away with a hiss. 'It's a ring,' he observed.

Rex laid down with a huff and put his head on his front paws. 'I told you it was the cat,' he sighed.

The End

Quick, get to the next story!

Live and Die by Magic

The Realm of False Gods

A Short Story

Steve Higgs

Dedication

To lovers of Urban Fantasy everywhere.

Table of Contents:

More Books by Steve Higgs

Free Books and More

Hi there,

What is The Realm of False Gods?

A year in the making, this series of urban fantasy books takes the reader on a journey told through the eyes of multiple protagonists. Each of them has their own story laid out over several books. The stories overlap and intertwine as humanity races unknowingly toward a cataclysm from which there is no escape. A battle is coming, the Earth will need heroes.

Thousands of years ago, humanity was ruled over by a race of beings able to wield the Earth's source energy, the very power that makes the planet spin. They drew on it to power their magic and took humans as familiars. Their rule was benevolent; they brought balance and harmony to the planet, keeping all creatures, both magical and non-magical, in check. The humans worshiped them as gods.

For thousands of years they ruled unopposed, the mantle of supreme being passing down a single family line from father to son. Possessing stronger magic than any other, the supreme being also possessed ancient weapons and armour to ensure his invincibility. But an impatient son betrayed and murdered his father, releasing a death curse that split all magical creatures from the mortal realm.

Ungoverned, humanity thrived, and over time the magical beings and other creatures faded into legend, a legend that became known as religion.

But the magical beings were not dead. They were merely trapped on a parallel version of Earth, yearning to return and squabbling among themselves.

As the 21st Century gets under way, some four thousand years after they were torn from the Earth, effects of the death curse are beginning to weaken. Soon it will fail completely. The False Gods are going to return, some have already begun to find their way through. They bring their magic with them and they expect to rule again.

No one knows about them. No one is ready. But there are a few things these false gods don't know.

February 2014

Paris, France

Ambush

With an unnecessary flourish, I used my right hand to control the air. In my left, I held my trusty broken compass, using the air I conjured to direct my tracking spell. The wooden compass needle spun a little before settling on a direction, and then I started moving, following where it pointed as I raced across the stone plaza in front of the Louvre.

It was my first time in Paris, not that I was going to get to see much of it, and it had been drizzling steadily since I arrived as if the French capital disapproved of my presence here. The temperature was only just above freezing, cold enough to penetrate if a person was outside for long enough, which I already had been. The rain wasn't helping, and my hands were half-frozen because I couldn't conjure with gloves on. I wasn't wearing a hat either, so my ears and head were getting cold as the rain hit my scalp. Years ago, I wore my dark brown hair long, but in defiance of my ability to wield magic, my hairline receded in my late twenties. Nowadays I had a buzz-cut because of its practicality, the hair on my head roughly the same length as my five-day stubble.

A call from Deputy Commissioner Bliebtreu brought me here earlier today, his forces were stretched too thin to cover what might be a singular event he said, but he believed there was *something* here if I had time to check it. Things were quiet in my home city of Bremen, those from the immortal realm too wise to go there now I was back to defend it, so I got in my car and drove the eight hundred kilometres in one go, stopping only to relieve myself and grab refreshments to eat in the car. The journey took all day, so it was late evening now, and I was already tired but Bliebtreu hadn't been wrong; there was something here.

Night was upon the city, dark shadows from the streetlights made my silhouette appear freakish as I ran down stone steps toward the Seine and away from the tourists still gathered outside the famous museum.

Something had been taking children; three in four days, each of the parents reporting an intense cold sensation before they lost consciousness. They awoke with their child missing and all the terrible emotion that would invoke. I spoke with only one set of parents, the ones whose child was taken last night, their number passed to me by Bliebtreu. I took his word for it that the others reported the same story. They were all attacked in the street with no witnesses to report seeing anything.

I worried for what that meant because there was only one creature I knew of able to operate like that and they were all dead, hunted to extinction by the demons several thousand years ago because even they couldn't stomach that level of evil.

If you are wondering who I am, then the answer is Otto Schneider. I'm a wizard. My abilities came when I was fourteen, scaring the pants off me because I could suddenly do all manner of things that I shouldn't be able to do. I watched my parents for weeks, trying to carefully word a question so I could ask if they were like me without telling them what I was suddenly like. I felt certain they were not and, in the end, after observing them constantly, I accepted that it was just me.

Slowly, and very privately, I trained myself, experimenting with what I could do and learning, mostly from failure, what I could not. I can control elemental magic, which is to say that I can conjure air, water, and earth, and manipulate them to create fire and lightning and ice and steam and all manner of other useful effects. I went through the thirty milestone a while back but haven't aged since 2012 when... well, that's a story for another time, but I am stuck permanently in my early thirties and that suits me just fine.

One of the tools I developed was a tracking spell, which I was using right now to find Jean Dujardin, a four-year-old boy snatched twenty-six hours ago. I suspected I was already too late for the two children snatched previously.

Hurrying onwards, running along the bank of the river and drawing odd looks from tourists out despite the weather, my second sight picked up the familiar glow of a supernatural aura ahead. This was almost certainly the creature that took the child, but a glance at my compass confirmed I was still a long way from the boy I was tracking. That could mean only one thing: the monster wasn't in the same place as the child. This could be good or bad; the one thing my tracking spell wouldn't do was tell me what condition the target was in; all too often, it led me to a body. Whatever the case, tonight I would get to fight the creature without the child in the way and that would give me a free hand to unleash my full arsenal.

I slowed to a walk as I slid the compass back into a pocket. I would want both hands to deal with what I was about to find. Ahead of me was a bridge over the river and behind the concrete structure, as it formed the first arch into the water, was whatever was throwing off the aura. I couldn't tell what it was. It could be a demon or a shilt or what I hoped it wasn't for all I knew. It could even be something new, but whatever it was, it was about to get both barrels. Metaphorically speaking.

Closing the distance, I could see that whatever was there hadn't moved yet, but it was hiding in the shadows just the other side of the bridge as if waiting to ambush the next person coming through. Well, it was about to get a big surprise then.

Pulling ley line energy into my core from the fat line running through the centre of Paris and under the Louvre, I conjured moisture in the air, agitating it to create static electricity. Lightning was one of my most devastating spells, one which I had learned to control with deadly accuracy over the last few years. I could follow that up with fire, or ice or whatever the situation called for depending on what I found.

It was still there, just at the edge of the bridge, clearly ready to leap out the moment I emerged from beneath the concrete arch. It didn't get the chance.

As my right foot took the next step, the one that would bring the hidden figure into sight, I swivelled toward it, dropped to one knee and pushed the spell. From above my head, lightning arced; a blinding fork that ripped through the air with a deafening blast. Whatever it hit would need to have some serious magical muscle to stay conscious and was likely to get thrown several metres when the electricity earthed.

So it was to my great surprise when the lightning hit what appeared to be a giant shield, shaped like an ancient knight's, and earthed directly into the ground.

A growl was all the warning I got before the creature in the darkness leapt. It was coming right at me, moving fast and full of deadly intent. I was barely able to switch spells fast enough to stop it hitting me. Conjuring air instinctively because it is my most versatile spell, I caught the figure in mid-air just a metre from my face.

Its red eyes glowed in the dark, the mouth beneath them drawn back into an angry sneer. The air spell wasn't going to hold it for long, and I hadn't allowed for the reach of its arms which even now were swinging in to smash my head.

At the last moment, just before I pushed fire from my right hand directly into its face and just a split second before a clubbing hand would impact the side of my skull, we both stopped.

The red behind the eyes staring at me dimmed and the face split into a grin. 'Wizard?'

Old Friends

'Zachary?' I hadn't seen the big, stupid, snarky d-bag of a werewolf in years. Not that I thought he was dead, but I hadn't heard anything about him for so long, he had slipped from my memory. Looking at him now, I had to admit I forgot just how big and imposing he is. Standing over two metres tall, he was as broad across his shoulders and chest as two average men and like me, his age was frozen in time. Unlike me, he was still in his twenties when it happened, but some guys get all the luck. His hairstyle had changed but that was about it. 'Why were you about to ambush me?' I asked.

'Ambush you?' His forehead wrinkled as he tried to work out what I meant. Then, when he looked back at where he had been in hiding behind the bridge, he sniggered. 'I was taking a leak, dummy. Why would I want to ambush you? It's not like I need the element of surprise to beat you, puny wizard.'

It amazed me how he slipped so easily back into being a dickhead after almost a decade. I didn't bother to retort, there was little to gain from engaging in a battle of wits, other than to encourage even more abuse from him. I was close to one meter ninety tall, hardly short for a man and I wasn't skinny either, yet Zachary always referred to me as if my proportions were childlike. For him, everyone was small by comparison and he liked to remind them as often as possible. He wore a permanent uniform of work boots, the Timberland style ones, jeans, and a t-shirt or vest. He ought to be freezing but something about his supernatural nature kept the cold at bay, so he never wore a coat. Tonight, his white t-shirt was stuck to his skin, the rain soaking the cotton, but it was probably a deliberate effect on his part as it did a great job of framing his pecs and his shaggy blonde hair, which I looked at with a hint of jealousy, was longer than before and styled with some kind of waterproof product to make him look like he was about to audition for a boy band. The clean-shaven jawline just made him look even younger than he was.

Pushing all that to one side, I asked a question. 'What was that shield thing?'

He waggled his eyebrows. 'You mean this?' He took a step back and brought up his left arm like a knight might if carrying a shield and the thing that deflected my lightning sprang into existence. I could tell it was ethereal; constructed of magic, not matter, but it looked solid enough. Answering a question I had yet to ask, he said, 'I picked it up in Croatia.'

'Croatia? What were you doing there?'

'This and that. Mostly avoiding those dicks from the Alliance who still think I should join them. I was in Mostar a while ago and a priest gave it to me. It's part of some ancient suit of armour. A couple of demons saw it and went nuts, saying something about this being the shield of God. I don't know whether it is... was, but the priest said it was found when the city got bombed back in the nineties. The church got damaged and this was found hidden inside a column. Everyone who touched it died instantly so they carefully tipped it into a box and sealed it up. I had a problem to sort out for them and the priest asked if I wanted to use it. I guess he knew enough about me to know it couldn't kill me.'

'What does it do?' I asked. 'Other than earth my lightning spell instantly.'

'It defends me. When I first touched it, it bonded with me or something. It was a piece of metal, but when I gripped it, it changed form, flowing into me and now, when I want it, all I have to do is imagine it on my arm and, hey presto, good magical word that, it appears. It also comes out by itself though, sensing attack and defending me. It was useful in Croatia when the demons came because it deflects hellfire.'

I stuck out my bottom lip and nodded, impressed. It was a fancy piece of hardware.

'What's with you anyway. This is a very different outfit to the one you were in last time I saw you. Back then you looked like a librarian; all tweeds jackets with leather elbow patches. Now you look like you slay vampires for a living.'

I looked down at what I was wearing. His jibe about my clothes was all nonsense, of course. I had never even owned a jacket with leather elbow patches, but I did dress more sedately back then. 'I spent some time in the immortal realm and I seem to do a lot more fighting than I used to back when we first met. These clothes are just more practical and hardwearing.'

I had on a pair of army boots, or what might pass for army boots, I suppose. They were comfortable and practical and didn't fall off in a fight like a pair of leather loafers once did. My trousers were black, rip-stop material designed for combat and I wore a long leather coat because it was easy to move in plus I liked the way it trailed behind me like a cape when I ran. Okay, I might have seen *Blade* one time too many.

'What are you doing in Paris?' he asked, doing whatever it was that he did to make the shield go away and then starting to walk along the path.

He was going the direction I needed to go, his 'ambush' temporarily distracting me from my quest to find the missing boy. As I took the compass from my pocket again, I said, 'I could ask you the same thing.'

'I asked first,' he countered.

Pausing briefly while I checked my direction, he waited for me until I started moving again. 'There's something here,' I murmured absentmindedly, wondering again if it was going to be the thing I didn't want it to be. 'Something that took a child earlier today.'

He stopped and placed a hand on my chest to stop me. 'Do you know what it is?' He was being serious for once, not something I got from him very often in the past.

'I might. Why?'

He started walking again. 'I caught sight of it two nights ago. I chased it for over a kilometre, but I lost it in the rooftops near Notre Dame. Whatever it is, it's unfriendly and it is fast, and it fires some kind of barbs from its face.'

I hung my head. I knew what it was for sure now. 'It's a whyker.'

The Whyker

'Are you tracking it?' Zachary asked. He had seen my broken compass before and knew what I used it for.

I shook my head. 'No. The boy. A four-year-old called Jean Dujardin.'

Zachary's face was an angry mask suddenly. 'Four-years-old? This thing deserves to die. What did you call it?'

'A whyker. I didn't think there were any left. I only heard about them in legends told by the demons. They ended up trapped in the immortal realm along with all the other magical creatures and the demons hunted them to extinction. If that's what this is, then we are in trouble.'

'That's hardly hero talk, wizard. Don't be such a worrier. You've got the werewolf back on your side tonight. It won't stand a chance.'

I wasn't so certain. 'From what I heard, it took dozens of demons to kill just one of these things.'

Turning around to walk backwards so he could look at me, he asked, 'Does it have magical testicles?' I raised one eyebrow at him. 'Didn't think so. One kick to the spuds and it'll drop like anything else.'

He always had a joke, but this was a serious situation. 'We need a plan, Zac. We can't just run at it and shout insults.'

He considered that for a second. 'How about this? I throw myself at it and while it's wearing itself out trying to eat me to death, you stick some lightning up its butt and explode it from the inside?'

Ignoring him, I looked down at the compass and up again. 'We need to get across the river.'

'It's there!' yelled Zachary, breaking into a run. 'Last one there is a children's entertainer.' Ignoring yet another jibe about my particular set of skills, I tracked where he had been looking, squinted and then, remembering myself, I closed and reopened my eyes, bringing my second sight into play. I didn't need to close my eyes to do it, but it made it easier and I got a headache if I didn't.

I saw it instantly, a glowing golden aura rising out of the water of the Seine on the far bank. Seventy metres ahead of me was a bridge we could use to get across. Zachary was already there, his speed not something I could ever hope to match. I had a few tricks of my own though, one of which was particularly appropriate for this occasion.

'Ha! Beat me now, wolfman,' I muttered to myself as I faced the water and held out my arms. Using an air spell to provide lift, I glanced around, saw that there were hundreds of people who would see me and lifted myself off the ground anyway. The first few times I had tried to reverse engineer my air conjuring to give me flight had not gone very well. I crashed a lot, but I got the idea when I saw another wizard do it with finesse. Knowledge that it could be done plus a lot of practice resulted in enough confidence to do it now.

I flew upright, looking graceful as I crossed high above the river, and making sure Zachary saw me as I passed him. He was running flat out, moving faster than an Olympic sprinter, but I was still going to get there first. He frowned at me and mouthed something that would not be printable, then he gave me the bird for good measure.

The whyker was out of the water and long gone by the time I touched down on Ile de la Cité, a small island sitting in the middle of the Seine and famous for being the home of Notre Dame. It made sense that the whyker was here somewhere. Churches always sat on the most powerful ley lines, which was why creatures from the immortal realm so often chose to cross through near them. Notre Dame is huge and ancient, the ley line beneath it bigger and more ancienter. I tried to correct the word in my head but couldn't work out quite how it should go.

'Did you see which way it went?' asked Zachary, arriving next to me a few seconds after I touched down. He was jogging on the spot, all pumped up and ready for a fight, looking about for any sign of the creature.

I shook my head, checking the compass one last time before putting it away. 'No. The boy is here though. Less than fifty metres from us. This is good and bad.'

'You know how I love it when you are cryptic, wizard,' grumbled the werewolf as he started to strip off his clothes. Not that he was wearing much, a t-shirt, jeans and a pair of work boots; his usual outfit regardless of the weather. The t-shirt was soaked through, but he took everything off and folded his clothes neatly, placing them under a bush in the vain hope they might be safe there until he returned.

Cat calls and whistles came from a party boat going by on the river as women caught sight of his lean muscular frame and naked butt. He turned to give them the shot they were calling for and then transformed into a werewolf right before their eyes to scare the living crap out of them. One second he was a naked man, the next he was a terrifying beast. He was tall for a human, but once transformed, he stood upright on his back legs to reach a height of two and a half metres. The change left him man shaped except for his wolf head and wolf hands. Not that his hands became paws; they were still hands but far bigger than before and each digit ended with a fifteen-centimetre claw. The claws made it hard to grip things, though not impossible. Otherwise, he looked like a man wearing a convincing costume as his white skin became almost black and sprouted course black hair. His blue eyes now glowed a deep, dark red inside his skull and a golden glow emanated from inside his skin in thin lines like his veins were filled with liquid gold. He was terrifying to look at but also nowhere near as scary as some things I had seen.

Humans, normal people that is, were now almost all aware on some level that supernatural creatures really did exist. The proliferation of good quality cameras built into everyone's phone guaranteed there would always be someone around to capture an event and there had been lots over the last decade or so as the demons began to push their way into the mortal realm. Tonight was no exception, so as the screams of horror subsided, phones came out.

Zachary turned to give them three-quarter profile and howled dramatically for the cameras.

'Was that entirely necessary?' I asked when the ship was passing from sight and he finally stopped doing muscle poses.

'Necessary? Of course not,' he growled, his naturally deep voice now just a touch deeper and a little more growly. 'I think they liked the show though. Besides, hiding what we are and letting them pretend we don't exist won't do them any favours when the curse finally breaks. Demons will come to enslave all these good people and I don't think you and I can stop them. They need to be ready.'

He was right, of course; we had talked about it before. No one knew when the death curse would fail, not even the angels and demons, but we knew it was coming and when it happened, the Earth would be changed forever. 'It's not just you and me, Zac,' I told him. 'There are others who will face them with us.'

'I know,' he sighed, twisting his head side to side as if limbering up. 'Did you see the thing on the news in Chippewa Falls? I had to look up where that is, but the story has demon stamped all over it. Someone there beat it.'

I nodded. I had seen it and I knew the Alliance were trying to find out who was there for them to recruit. 'Bliebtreu and the Alliance are trying to pull some of us together into a force that might be able to fight them.'

'The Alliance,' he scoffed. 'They can all go f...' suddenly he wasn't standing next to me anymore. I caught a faint glimpse of his shield manifesting, but it went with him as he flew backwards out of sight.

I whispered, 'Cordus,' to power my barrier spell, an invisible shield of my own design materialising just in time to stop the next giant barb from hitting me. Behind me, I heard a splash as Zachary hit the river.

The barb had caught the curved edge of my shield, glancing off rather than driving me back into the river, but it jarred my whole arm and made it feel numb. All around me, the lights were going out, plunging the area into darkness. It was a trick I had seen others perform though I had not yet worked out how it was done. Twenty metres ahead of me was a road running along the outside edge of the island. Cars were screeching to a stop and horns were blaring as the whyker walked in front of them, blocking the street and causing crashes. Panicked screams filled the air as those with any sense abandoned their cars and ran.

Behind and to my left, a barge designed for taking people along the river was moored. I heard yells to get clear as they too spotted the approaching monster and ran for their lives.

'Wizard,' the whyker hissed, its voice like a skeleton's bones being rattled together. I had only ever heard stories, I hadn't even seen pictures, but the descriptions didn't do this thing justice. It was nothing short of an abomination, something the Earth's source energy created at the dawn of time specifically to power nightmares for the rest of all eternity.

It was five times my size, maybe three metres high and four metres long, and it resembled a scorpion, less the tail, with a spider's head. Its body looked like chitinous plates, a hard exoskeleton that shone with the rain and streetlights. Multiple eyes stared at me, sizing me up as it considered which bit of me to eat first. Its voice came to me without the need for a mouth that could form words, the sounds arriving in my head unbidden and in my own language, a magic of some kind translating it.

'You are about to perish, wizard. Why did you come here?'

I wanted to stall for as long as I could. I had heard Zachary surface already. No other creature on the planet can string together that many expletives and somehow still make a coherent sentence. Together we might still be no match for this thing, but I certainly didn't want to take it on alone.

I answered its question. 'I came for the child. Is he alive?'

'Yes,' hissed the whyker. 'Though not for long. The child possesses what I need to sustain myself in this mortal realm. Soon I will consume him and look for another.'

I stepped forward, conjuring the earth as I closed the distance between us, my strides showing a confidence I didn't feel. Readying my spell, I snarled, 'I'm afraid not. I am here to stop you.'

'One mortal wizard? You will die painfully.' It moved suddenly, just as I unleashed my spell. While it was talking, I had been pushing my senses down into the ground beneath its feet. It was standing part on the grass of the riverbank and part on the road. Gathering the earth in my mind, I planned to rip out a wide circle of it and flip it upside down to pin the monster in place while I worked my next spell. I thought I could probably kill it if I had it in one place for long enough, but before I could make any attempt to trap it, it leapt.

It went high into the air above me, planning to land right where I stood. My barrier spell would deflect the initial blow but would then collapse at which point the monster would skewer me most effectively.

Trying to judge it right so I wouldn't go for a swim, I conjured air to shoot myself back out over the river. The whyker landed where I had been standing a heartbeat before and I hit it with fire, a white-hot lance that would burn through steel given a few seconds. Unfortunately, I couldn't sustain it for that long. Even with years of training, I can only conjure one spell at a time and my upwards trajectory had already been corrected by gravity. I either switched back to an air spell or I went for a swim in the Seine.

The whyker had magic of its own I discovered as it raised itself onto its rear two sets of legs and created a ball of what looked like hellfire with the front pair. I didn't hang around to find out if it was hellfire but went higher and then over the top of it. Flying using an air spell isn't like you might imagine: all smooth and graceful. Even with years of practice, it is jerky and precarious. I'm never entirely certain if I will break my legs when I land, and I cannot very easily conjure any other spell while I am falling. On the ground is better, so, I picked a spot and made sure I landed in cover, placing a thick, raised ornamental flowerbed between me and it.

It had shot several blasts at me as I flew over its head, each of them missing, but now that I was easier to pinpoint, the next one hit the flowerbed I cowered behind. An explosion of pulverised brick and ancient mortar peppered me with shards of stone. I ran across the street to get some more distance, keeping low so it wouldn't see me and hid around the corner of a building.

As I glanced back out, the beast fired into the raised flowerbed again, blowing it to smithereens. Instinctively, I ducked away from it, the werewolf's voice reaching my ears the next second. 'Will you get up, wizard? You're embarrassing me.'

'Will you take some cover?' I hissed. 'That thing's got a cannon.'

He shook his head, never taking his eyes off the whyker. 'There might be girls watching,' he explained as he puffed out his chest.

The whyker was coming our way. While I cowered and coughed in the dust kicked up by the exploding flowerbed, Zachary stood in the road willing the creature to come at him.

Then I heard a siren and stole a glance around the corner of the building. From behind the monster, a single police cruiser had just entered the street. There were more sirens of course, the cops reacting as they undoubtedly received multiple calls, but they were all still too distant to be of immediate concern.

The unfortunate fellows in the car down the street never stood a chance, the whyker barely even bothering to look before it fired a bolt of hellfire directly at the car. It exploded in a ball of flame before Zachary or I could move. There was just no way we could have stopped it.

There was openly expressed rage in his voice when Zachary's grumbling bass reached my ears, 'Come along, wizard. I think it high time we introduced ourselves.'

Taking a second to catch my breath, I pushed away from the wall and stood up. There were two of us against a ridiculous beast powered by a stronger magic than I could hope to wield. Earth's source energy, the strongest source of magic, didn't bother with measly ley lines, it tapped right into the core power of the planet and no human could survive channelling that much juice. Despite the werewolf's cockiness, we were about to get our asses whooped.

Zachary didn't care about any of that though. He stood in the street and faced it down. 'Sorry, old chap, we seem to have gotten off on the wrong foot. You've probably heard of us. I'm the ass-kicking werewolf who is about to tear your head off and make you eat it.' I ran the picture of that in my head and couldn't make it work no matter what I did. He wasn't finished though. 'My little friend isn't hiding,' he hissed at me out of the side of his mouth, 'stop hiding, wizard.' Then went back to his previous volume. 'He's getting ready with a really big magic trick.' I sighed at his deliberate choice of phrase. He insisted on talking about me as if I was about to pull a rabbit from a hat or vanish in a puff of smoke. 'I'm giving you five seconds to die on the spot of your own volition. After that, we're going to make you regret being born.'

'I'm getting hungry,' the whyker's voice echoed in my head. 'Your feeble attempts at magic will do nothing but briefly delay my meal. Time for you to die so I can feast.' Then it let loose with a barrage of hell fire and the sharp barbs which it shot from holes either side of its mouth. It was like spitting out its own teeth, but they were the size of beers cans and moving at the speed of bullets, each of them powerful enough to punch a hole through a wall.

Zachary stood his ground, hunkered down behind his shield, or maybe that *should* be God's shield given the way it protected him. The hellfire blasts hit it and simply dissipated, fizzling down to nothing as if the shield was absorbing them. However, the barbs were something the shield hadn't been designed to deal with. He didn't let their energy push him back though, he held the shield in place, refusing to yield so each one clanged into the shield and ricocheted off to hit a wall or a car. Half of them then penetrated what they hit to a depth of twenty centimetres. The ones that hit the cars went right through.

Shouting at the monster from behind his shield, he said, 'I'm about to count to five. Then you're in big trouble.' Angered by his defiance, the whyker doubled the barrage, shunting Zachary back half a metre despite his attempt to stay put.

How the hell were we going to beat this thing?

'Are you planning to play along, wizard?' asked Zachary in the same tone he might use to ask someone directions. 'I'm getting ready to kick it in the nuts and could use a distraction.'

I had no idea what he had in mind, but I could do a distraction easily enough. There was lots of water nearby and it was already cold out, so I chose to hit the big, ugly, magical brute with ice. It's a simple spell, and water is easy to manipulate.

Reaching out to the river, I pushed my senses into the frigid water and began a maelstrom beneath the surface that erupted upward in a waterspout. Then, switching spells, I conjured air, twisting it into a tornado that spun in a tight funnel above the water, drawing it up into the night sky. I stretched it until it reached over fifty metres in height, then focused my effort into dropping the temperature, taking the millions of litres of near-freezing water just a few degrees colder. Suddenly I had ten thousand icicles just hanging in the air.

They weren't hanging for long.

I yanked them downwards, sending wave after wave of deadly frozen spears at the whyker's head. I doubted they would do him much harm, even if I did mentally label them as deadly. However, they were enough to distract him as Zachary asked.

The whyker didn't see the ice coming. The first few icicles smashed into its head and body, but as expected, their effect was minimal and the damage they did was nil. The ice exploded into millions of pieces on impact, showering the street with ice crystals though the whyker ignored them as one might ignore the buzzing of flies.

I had only used about one percent of the available ice so far though, so I gritted my teeth and threw the next fifty percent in one go. Sheer volume was one thing the whyker couldn't ignore, the constant barrage began to pummel it to the ground, and it was being slowly buried as the smashed ice built up around it.

Angry that we continued to challenge it, the creature switched its attention to the ice, attempting to avoid it but finding I could follow it wherever it might go. The moment it was distracted, Zachary came out from behind his shield, breaking into a sprint as he charged toward the monster. I swear I heard him shout, 'Five,' as he barrelled down the street. I had no idea what he planned to do but I diverted the rest of the ice back into the river so I wouldn't hit my ally with it, then pulled in more ley line energy and attacked the whyker with fire, shooting over Zachary's head at the monster's ugly face.

Zachary reached the ice and threw himself onto it, sliding on his right shoulder as he held his left arm up. At the end of his arm were five sharp claws, one extending from each finger like five daggers. The lack of friction on the icy road carried him between the creature's front legs just as it saw him. It recognised the danger but couldn't do anything about it.

Was there a vulnerable spot on its underbelly?

No. There wasn't.

I saw Zachary's claws clip the creature's legs and underside as he slid through to pop up behind it, but nothing happened. The whyker didn't howl in pain, viscera didn't fall out to douse the street in awful black lumpy liquid. It didn't even really seem to care about the fire hitting its face. I had wondered how on earth the two of us might beat a creature it took a platoon of demons to kill. The answer appeared to be that we couldn't. The only advantage we gained from our last move was that now its attention appeared to be drawn in two different directions.

Zachary shouted to me, 'Wizard, we have a problem. This thing doesn't have any testicles. I think it might be a girl.' Even now, when it was about to mush him into the ground, he was still making jokes.

As if annoyed by his comments, the whyker spun about on the spot, attacking Zachary with its front legs, grabbing for him with its pincers. God's shield came into play, defeating the creature every time it lunged for him, so it switched to forming hellfire which it flung at him. That had the same effect, the two of them reaching an unhappy stalemate as the whyker did its best to kill him and Zachary refused to die. The tables had turned though, the creature was focused on Zachary, making him the distraction and leaving me with a free hand. The sensible move would be to run away at this point. Throwing all the power in the world at this thing didn't seem to have much impact; I couldn't see a way to defeat it, but something occurred to me as I dithered over which spell to try next.

Rope a Dope

So far, we had tried magic and little else. It was a magical creature and probably thousands of years old which made it very powerful and very experienced in using magic to defend or attack. However, given a second to think, my brain flashed to several occasions when I caught out demons and other creatures by dropping the magic to punch them in the face instead. They never expected it, always too reliant on magic to consider any other form of attack likely.

I needed to try the same trick with this thing, but I needed something bigger than my fist to do it with. I saw what I wanted, but I couldn't get it from where it was all the way to where I needed it, I just didn't have that kind of power. The obvious alternative was to get the whyker to go closer to it. It wasn't going to voluntarily play chase though, so I needed something it would follow. Like...

The boy.

It admitted it needed the boy to sustain it in this realm. I didn't know if it was any boy it needed or one with some kind of special qualities, but it had come back to this island for it. I stopped debating the concept internally and started running. The compass came out of my pocket just as I conjured the tracking spell. I had an item of the boy's clothing to use as a focus, the spell telling me he was very close now.

'Zachary!' I yelled to get his attention as the whyker continued to pummel him. He was down on one knee, the shield above his head as the monster did its best to smash him into the ground. It was beginning to succeed I saw, the tarmac around the werewolf beginning to crack and crumble. 'I'll be right back,' I shouted. 'I need to get something.'

I got an incredulous expression in response and Zachary shouted something unrepeatable in my direction as I ran up Rue Aubé and away from the action. His words carried on the air as he bellowed after me, promising to give my mother something to hang her bathrobe on. I wasn't entirely certain what that might be, but I had a good idea.

I felt a desperate sense of urgency; the whyker wasn't stupid and might decide to explore where I had gone. My plan relied on getting it to the water, not drawing it further inland.

The boy was close. I could tell that much because the compass was pulling now as it always did when the focus got near to the target. To my right was a large building, some kind of commercial business but it was centuries old, the walls made from rough-hewn rock, not formed house bricks. The boy was somewhere inside, and I thought that was going to be a problem until I spotted an iron gate leading to steps which descended below the building. I thought the compass was trying to take me inside, but it was merely indicating toward the middle of the building, a position I could just as easily reach by going under. Not only that, the dark passage looked like the place a monster would hide a frightened child.

The gate was open, which I suppose it had to be unless the whyker had obtained a key from somewhere. However, as I looked more closely, I could see that the gate itself was intact. The piece on the wall where it should latch onto had been ripped away, the anchor bolts torn out of the rock. I paused; if the door was open, why hadn't the child escaped? Even a four-year-old could climb some steps. Unless the whyker had already killed him.

I steeled myself for what I might find and descended into the darkness, conjuring a flame into my hand to light the way. 'Jean,' I called, trying to make my voice sound friendly, certain the poor child was down here and terrified in the dark. 'Jean.'

I heard a small sound of movement, like a foot moving on a dusty floor and then I saw him, my second sight picking up his aura. It was weak, but it was there; the child possessing some supernatural ability even if it was years away from manifesting. His clothes were dirty, and his face was streaked with tears, but he was unharmed so far as I could see. He was held to the wall with a gluey secretion, far too strong for the boy to break free by himself, but it snapped and came apart the moment I got my hands on it. He didn't know who I was, and my French was about as good as his German, but he clung to me like a spider monkey on its mother as I climbed back up the steps to the street.

Just before I exited onto the pavement outside, I paused again. The passageway leading down was less than a metre and a half across. How did the whyker get down there to deposit the child? I couldn't ask Jean and even if we did speak the same language, I couldn't be sure he would be able to give me a clear picture. It didn't matter though; I was certain the whyker had been down there; how else could it have stuck Jean to the wall?

The question rattled around in my head but a crash from the direction of the river made me pick up the boy and run. I felt certain carrying the terrified child to where he would see his monster again was a bad idea; I was going to use him as bait and that wasn't fair. I did it though, accepting that I had no time for anything else and a definite need to protect the next child the creature might snatch if I didn't stop it now.

I was running when I hit the corner, firing lightning bolts at the back end of the creature to get its attention. I made sure it could see me with the child, but my eyes were drawn to Zachary. I had worried about him, worried about leaving him to fend off the beast by himself but once again, he proved how close to invincible he was.

I expected him to be half buried in the ground, pounded flat like a steak, but I couldn't have been more wrong. He had the shield on his left forearm and was twirling a lamppost in his right hand. As the monster twitched its head around to see where the sparks arcing over its back end came from, Zachary darted in to smash the lamppost into the side of its head.

It flinched from the blow, demonstrating how much power the werewolf was able to put into it, but its focus was already on me. It had seen Jean and it wanted him.

Above all, I needed to keep Jean safe. He hadn't seen the whyker yet, his head was tucked over my shoulder, so as I faced the monster, he faced away from it. That was about to change though as I ran away.

Jean stiffened instantly as he saw the monster again, and though I cooed for him to close his eyes, his little hands dug in to hold on for dear life as the whyker screamed in anger and charged after me. I didn't have far to go, but I wasn't sure I could make it even with a decent lead. The werewolf came to my rescue again. As the whyker turned around to chase me, Zachary leapt at him, driving the lamppost up into the air and then down again. The tattered edge, where he tore it from the ground, came down where two chitinous plates joined and he finally got through its armour.

It bellowed in rage, turning around on itself to swipe a giant front arm which caught Zachary across his ribs. He flew across the street, swept sideways to crunch against a building.

He would get back up but not soon enough for the last part of this. I planned to end it now and Zachary had just bought me the time to get in position. At the water's edge, I slowed and turned to face the monster. Jean still clung to me and I had to prise his fingers away from my neck as I set him down on the pavement behind me. He wouldn't let go completely, clinging to my left leg and hiding behind me, but it was now or never as the whyker stalked towards us.

'That's mine,' its words echoed in my head.

'Come and get him, monster,' I growled back, my jaw set and my teeth clenched. What I was about to attempt ought to be possible, it just wasn't something I had ever tried before.

He was coming closer, unwilling to throw a barb at me or risk flinging hellfire for fear of hitting the child and depriving himself of his prize. That played into my hand, but I backed up a pace to give myself some more room as I drew in ley line energy hungrily. I would need to channel more of it as I conjured the spell. There was no more time to ponder on the task though because it was at hand.

I reached into the Seine again, pushing my will deep into the water to gather a surge from the very bottom of the river. As the creature came level with it, I forced water up in a huge funnel, pushing the abandoned river barge upwards. I could feel the sheer magnitude of the task pushing back against me; I was trying to move so much mass it was making my jaw hurt.

It moved though, inexorably lifting above the surface on a giant water finger. I had to wait until the whyker came past it, as I didn't want him to see what I was doing. Fortunately, the sound from the barge itself was drowned out by the noise of approaching sirens.

'Did you really think you could stop me?' asked the whyker, it rattle-of-bones voice sounding in my head. I barely heard it over the noise of blood pumping between my ears as I grunted with the effort. I felt like collapsing to the floor, but I was close now, the barge almost ready to tip.

I planned to hit it with something it couldn't just magic away; a thousand tons of steel. Drop that on it and it would either be crushed to death instantly or be pinned in place, at which point I felt confident Zachary and I could finish it. I was wrong though, neither thing happened.

The beast was almost on the spot I had marked in my head when the tail end of the barge eclipsed the moon. The sudden change in light on the path gave the game away, the whyker whipping its head around to see what I had in store for it. I forced a last-ditch effort into the water and the barge flipped, toppling over to land top side down right on my aiming mark. Dirt, water, and muck from the bottom of the boat all slammed down and together with paving slabs exploded outwards with a force that was enough to make me stagger backwards. Carried on the air, the muck and water and everything else pelted me, and an orange buoy the size of a small car bounced by as it too made a break for freedom.

The barge had landed right where the monster had been.

It wasn't there any more though, it had seen the danger coming and escaped.

In many ways this was a better result because its method of escape was to shrink. It had some shifting ability in its genetics somewhere which explained how it had been able to move around Paris freely enough to steal children and how it had been able to fit down the tight passage to hide the boy.

It was my size now and I experienced a swell of confidence as I lifted my arms to ready the next spell. Now it was smaller, I planned to explode it from the inside. It was something I had done before, even though it was disgusting to witness, but as I tried to conjure the spell, I sagged. I was done, half crippled from the effort of the previous spell. I needed a chocolate bar and a lie down, but the beast was already beginning to grow again.

I screamed at myself in defiance of my own weakness, filled with rage that I could come so close and yet be defeated.

'Shall I save you again?' asked the werewolf, as he gripped the whyker's head and ripped it clean off. 'Told you,' he spat at the headless corpse.

From behind me as I leaned on my knees for support, four-year-old Jean whooped with joy and finally let go of my leg, running to hug Zachary instead.

The monster's body hung in the air for a second or so and then collapsed to the ground where it leaked ugly dark liquid onto the path. Considering the destruction around us, I doubted a little more muck to clean up was going to be of much concern. The rain continued to fall steadily, mixing with the goop to wash it toward a drain. Flashing blue and red lights bounced off the surface of the water as cop cars came over the bridge. Yet more of them were approaching along the edge of the island, driving on the pavement and grass to get around the abandoned cars. They would arrive soon, shouting orders and getting excited. Zachary wouldn't hang about for that, he never did, and I wondered when I might see him again.

The monster was dead, and the boy was safe, those were the things that mattered. I would do my best to tidy up the mess, putting the barge back into the water while hoping a call from Bliebtreu would smooth things over with the authorities here. It wasn't as if they could hold me, I was too powerful for that.

Right now though, I felt utterly exhausted. Choosing to stop fighting it, I lowered myself to the ground and sat in a puddle. I was soaked anyway.

Zachary, still looking like a two and half metre-tall werewolf, had Jean on his shoulders like a dad at a Sunday soccer game, both his hands held up so Jean could hold onto them. When he caught my eye, he said, 'I know I've said it before, wizard, but...'

I wafted a hand for him to stop talking. 'I know. I know. I'm such a disappointment.'

The End

Still one to go!

Zombie Granny

Blue Moon Investigations

A Short Story

Steve Higgs

I was on my way back to the office when my phone rang. The car system picked it up, the screen advising that the caller was James, my newly employed and very LGBT admin assistant.

'Good afternoon, James.'

'Tempest, I have a client at the office, will you be long?'

'About another five minutes. What sort of case is it?' I was asking if he considered it a real case i.e. there was a crime to investigate or mystery to solve or was the case a questionable one. I got a lot of the latter. Just yesterday a rather well-spoken lady wanted me to help rid her of a plague of gnomes that were ruining her lawn. It's *definitely* not moles she assured me. I didn't take the case.

'It is to do with the zombies.' James continued, excitement in his voice. When I first met James, he was part of a vampire-wannabe cult and I was still trying to convince him that everything supernatural was a load of baloney.

'James, we have been through this several times now. Do you remember what we agreed?'

'Erm.' He started. 'That there are no genuine cases, because there is no supernatural or paranormal and all the creatures like werewolves and vampires and pixies do not exist.'

'That's right, James. That is the entire premise of the business for which you work.'

'But isn't there some actual evidence to support the notion that the zombie legend, which was spawned by slaves in Haiti as they were worked to death by the French colonists, has some scientific grounding. Also, is it not true that the tetrodotoxin poison from the pufferfish can, in sub-lethal doses be used to create a state of suspended animation whereupon the person can be controlled?'

I said nothing for a few seconds, 'James, are you reading to me from Wikipedia?'

'Little bit.'

'Make some tea. I will be there soon.' I was supposed to be a private investigator available for hire to solve crimes, but a young lady at the paper that ran my first advert had misread my business and I had been marketed as a paranormal investigator. The phone had been in a constant state of agitation ever since, so perhaps I should be grateful to her. I was, however, regularly asked to investigate stupid nonsense. A recent case I took on started with the client claiming that her neighbour was a shape shifter - it turned out he was a cross dresser and entitled to be left alone. Another one, that thankfully I was bright enough to turn down, was from a man that assured me he had been cursed by his ex-wife and his todger no longer worked. Occasionally there was a genuine crime beneath the strange circumstances, but the more regular explanation was that the client was daft.

This would be my first zombie case, but I should have seen it coming. The first report of a zombie attack had occurred three days ago in Sevenoaks, a large village with a postcode price-tag high enough to warrant Ferrari opening a dealership there. The zombies had appeared just after lunchtime on a Thursday. They had attacked several shoppers in the village centre. The television and radio had gone crazy with various experts giving their thoughts on what had caused the outbreak.

The second and third incidents had occurred the following day, one in Gillingham and one in Canterbury, but not simultaneously. In all three cases, the number of zombies appearing was limited to a handful, but they were still wreaking havoc. In each case the ensuing panic appeared to have caused several local businesses to catch fire. I had watched the news last night where footage taken on a teenager's phone had been played. In the clip, which lasted about thirty seconds, a little old lady with a perfectly set, pastel-pink perm and matching coat had lunged directly at the phone. Her facial features were contorted, her eyes were utterly deranged, and a deep, guttural sound emanated from the back of her throat.

The footage had gone viral within a few hours, so the world was now talking about *zombie grandma*. She had lunged for and bitten the arm of a pretty teenage-girl. The girl screamed, but then realised that nothing much was happening as the little old lady simply gnawed at the sleeve of her jacket. Another bystander, a boy, shoved the old lady away and she tripped, fell backwards and landed hard on the pavement behind her. The camera zoomed in on the girl's arm where a top set of dentures were embedded. The chap holding the camera had been laughing uncontrollably as the girl screamed in disgust and shook her arm.

On the floor, the old lady was now beginning to cry in pain and was no longer making zombie noises. The news report claimed that she had broken her hip in the fall. The police had arrested her, I think mostly because they did not know what else to do and she had gone to hospital, restrained, and accompanied by several police officers. The report went on to show the Police at the scene where a spokesperson was surrounded by continuous camera flashes which illuminated the early evening gloom. Reading from what I assumed was a hastily prepared statement, he advised the microphones positioned beneath his chin that several persons displaying, as yet, unexplained violent behaviour had been detained for their own safety and that of the general populace. Also, several people had been bitten and admitted to hospital. He refused to engage on many of the rapidly fired questions, which all carried the same theme of whether this was, in fact, the start of a zombie plague.

I had watched the news with greater attention than I had ever given it. I was firmly in the camp that there was no paranormal explanation to anything. Zombies fell into this classification, but the footage was compelling and difficult to argue with. When the first attack had been reported, I had immediately labelled it as a hoax, perpetrated by actors.

What else could it be?

Now though I was not so sure. If it was actors, then they were really committed to the role. I had just taken on an additional investigator, Amanda Harper. She was a police officer and was still working out her notice period before coming to the business full time. This meant I had someone who could tell me what the media would not, so I knew the police has set up several special holding areas where they were still keeping the zombies they had already rounded up. She was able to confirm that they remained violently aggressive and kept trying to bite anyone that came near them. They showed no interest in food or water or anything else, but the police had been able to take identification from a few of them so now knew they had an eclectic mix of people. It included a primary school teacher, a lawyer, a truck driver, a single mum etcetera. Amanda had appeared genuinely scared when I spoke to her.

I parked around the back of my office and ran up the stairs to find James and an elderly gentleman sat in the two seats near the window that overlooks Rochester High Street. The client appeared to be at least seventy years old. He wore an ill-fitting grey suit that hung on his shrunken frame. His face was a map of thin, red lines surrounding sad and tired eyes. I introduced myself to quickly learn that he was the husband of the *zombie granny*.

The conversation was swift. The poor chap had not been allowed to see his wife nor speak with her since the incident. I understood that she was a key element to the police though. She was the only person who had been acting like a zombie and no longer was. He begged me to investigate what was going on and prove his wife was not a crazed creature lusting after human flesh and I accepted the case. He offered me his life savings, his house, whatever it took but I offered to do it for free. This was not something I had ever done before, but he looked like he had little money and I genuinely wanted to help.

The little old man departed, shuffling down the stairs from my office wearing a brave face. I sat down to arrange my thoughts.

James was hovering behind me. 'Do you have plans for the afternoon?' I asked. He only worked part time hours, six mornings a week.

'Actually, yes. I am seeing a hypnotist.' He paused, waiting for me to show signs of interest. When I did not, he pressed on anyway. 'So, I went to a show with some friends last week and I was hypnotised. Apparently, I have just the right type of mind for it...'

A bit weak and easily led then.

'...and I have been invited along to a special event today.' I continued to show no interest. 'No one else got invited.' His tone was pleading for me to make a comment.

I gave in and asked a question, 'Where is the event?'

He brightened instantly, 'Oh, it's just around the corner in The Casino Nightclub. I had better be off. I don't want to be late.' He grabbed his coat and scarf, bid me a pleasant weekend and headed out the door with a quick goodbye.

Amanda had emailed me a file last night which I had briefly inspected. The file listed the names of the zombies they had been able to identify thus far and provided interview notes from zombie grandma, whose real name was Edna Goodbridge. It also contained other notes they had been able to compile about the attacks, such as time and location of sightings, number of zombies involved and lots of other facts that did not seem all that helpful.

Edna had been treated for the pain and for her broken hip. Her age was recorded as seventy-two. The interview notes revealed almost nothing worthwhile. She had no memory of how she came to be in Sevenoaks. The previous evening she gone out for dinner with friends in Rainham town centre and had no memory beyond that. There was a line towards the end of the notes that caught my attention. The hospital reported that there were some traces of an unknown drug in her blood. They had sent it off for analysis. I filed the information away for future reference.

I started to make notes. An hour of intense Google searches later and I knew a lot more about zombies than I ever had and knew just about everything the police knew about the zombie appearances during the last few days. I stared at the handwritten pages, flicked a couple of them and reluctantly admitted that it meant *nothing*.

I scratched my head and made a cup of tea. *Ok. Let's try this from a different angle. If the people acting as zombies are not actually zombies, but are also not consciously playing at being them, then what are they? How does a person arrive at a state where they believe they are a zombie when they are not?*

I was stood next to the window idly stirring my tea when a possibility just popped into my head: *hypnotism.*

Could that work?

Galvanised into action, I dumped the tea, grabbed my jacket and ran around the corner to the occult bookshop owned by Frank Decaux. Frank was a connoisseur of all the weird stuff that I knew nothing about. He would be able to offer a unique perspective on what might be happening.

Bursting through his door I startled him, and he dropped an armful of gear he was carrying. It spilled over the floor, so I bent to help him pick it up. The first item I touched had its label towards me.

Zombie repellent.

I held it up, 'Really, Frank?'

'I can barely keep it on the shelf, Tempest. All the apocalypse protection gear is in high demand at the moment.'

'Okay.' I said to end that line of conversation. 'I need to ask you about hypnotism and whether it could be used to transform an audience into a zombie army?'

He stared at me incredulously, I had his attention.

'Well...'

'The short version please.' I pleaded. Frank had a habit of telling the listener the history, back story, origin story, alternate theories and how much he was selling books related to the subject for.

'Well, a good hypnotist can make a person do anything. These are real zombies though, Tempest. You must see that.' Frank would believe a paranormal explanation first every time.

I ignored him. 'How long would the hypnotic state last?'

'Well, I believe it depends on the individual. Some people are very hard to hypnotise because they resist the commands, but others could be placed into a hypnotic state perpetually I suppose. Alternatively, they could be triggered to act in a certain way by use of a code word until they were given a different one to revert back to their normal selves.'

I opened my mouth to ask a question, but it died on my lips as a scream from outside pierced the peaceful Saturday lunchtime. Frank and I froze and stared at each other for a brief moment, then sprang into action. We dropped the goods we were holding and rushed to the window. In the street below ought to be a scene of people sitting peacefully in cafés while others with places to go passed by and tourists or visitors poked around in shops. Instead, we were witness to a scene where almost everyone was now stationary. In the café windows, the faces were all looking out through the window rather than across the table at a companion. A base dread was forming a tight ball in my stomach. As I watched, I saw a man in the café get up from his seat and move towards the window to gain a better view. His seat tipped over backwards, but too distracted, he failed to even react as it slammed against the floor.

Then, like a switch being flipped, everyone started moving again. *In utter panic.*

I threw myself away from the window, across the bookstore and out into the street. The bookstore opened into a narrow side street so the main route through Rochester was to my left. In the aperture ahead of me, people were running by, all heading in the same direction. I reached the High Street and turned against the flow, towards the direction the people were running from.

Frank skidded to a halt behind me. I wanted to ask what he thought he was doing, but he had every right to be in the street with me. Despite the terror that gripped his face, I knew from recent experience that he had the heart of a lion. 'Ready?' I asked.

In answer, he showed me a back pack full of anti-zombie gear. The cans of zombie repellent surrounded several tubes of zombie bite relief cream, zombie armour, which was nothing more than shoulder pads, knee pads, and shin guards but spray painted black, some duct tape, heavy duty gloves and one item which I just had to take a closer look at. It was a small, black club with a handle, but it was the name written down the side in neon letters that had caught my attention

Zombie Twatting Stick.

I went to put it back, then changed my mind. I hefted it and swung it a couple of times. If I needed it, I assured myself. *Only* if I needed it.

Less than a minute had passed since we had heard the first scream and people were still charging down the street towards us.

'Get outta here.' A chap yelled to us as he went by us. I turned to see him go but we were already forgotten. Various screams, cries and questions regarding lost family members were audible over the general din.

I was angry. People were scared. This was my town, where I lived. It was no longer some report on television. I intended to find the people behind this mess and punch them. Hard.

Approaching down the street towards me were two people. I mentally re-classified them as zombies because I did not know what else I could call them. They were all classic-movie, shuffling feet, arms stretched out in front of them uttering a groaning, growling noise. One was a middle-aged man in a suit and tie, his slightly greying hair a little mussed and he had blood on his face. I could not tell if it was his or someone else's.

'Come on, Frank. Let's go introduce ourselves.' I suggested as I set off toward the pair.

He locked his eyes on us and drawled, 'Braiiinnns.'

His companion was a petite lady in her very early twenties or maybe younger. She wore no jacket against the cool October air and her stretchy top had been ripped so that her right, bra-clad boob poked out through the gap in the fabric.

She made a grab for a woman rushing by her and managed to snag her pony tail. Then she was all about trying to bite the poor woman.

Dashing forward, I used my zombie twatting stick to break the hot zombie chick's grip. Pony tail now free, the woman fled screaming and was gone. Frank meanwhile had pulled a can of anti-zombie spray from his backpack, fumbled to get the lid off and was spraying it at the zombie business guy in front of him.

It was silly string.

Having lost her prey the hot zombie chick had turned her attention to me. However, she weighed less than I can bicep curl, so I was keeping her at bay with one arm while dragging her towards Frank and the pack of gear. I was going to have to deal with zombie business guy first though.

'Behave.' I instructed hot zombie chick as she tried yet again to bend her neck enough to bite my arm. Zombie business guy lunged at Frank, but there was now so much silly string on his face it was obscuring his vision. If it bothered him, he showed no sign and made no attempt to remove it. Frank side stepped neatly and extended a foot to trip him.

Zombie business guy pitched forward, arms flailing and crashed down in a heap next to the bag of gear. Frank pounced on his back, pulling a wicked looking blade from his belt.

'Woah!' I yelled, still struggling with hot zombie chick. Frank was lifting his arms, preparing to drive the knife into the back of the man's head.

'Cut off the head or destroy the brain. It is the only way to kill them.' His voice a panicked shout.

His arms reached the apex of the swing and plunged downwards. I shoved hot zombie chick away and kicked Frank directly in his rib-cage. The blade missed its intended target and struck the pavement where it lodged between two cobblestones. I snatched it from his grip.

'Frank, they may look like zombies, they are behaving like zombies, but they are just plain, vanilla people under some kind of hypnotic spell.'

He stared at me, shocked that I had hit him and his gaze incredulous because I had prevented his first zombie kill. 'Look,' I said, grabbing hot zombie chick again before she could resume trying to bite me. 'Do zombies have a pulse? Check his pulse.'

It was a simple instruction and Frank placed his left hand on zombie business dude's neck. His face flushed with shock as his fingers felt the steady pump of blood beneath warm skin.

He nodded at me, confirming he understood. 'Duct tape.' I said simply and scooped two rolls from the discarded backpack. A few moments later, our two zombies had their hands taped securely behind their backs, their ankles bound, and several laps of tape had been wound around their heads and across their mouths. We manoeuvred them into a recessed shop doorway and left them. They both continued shaking their heads and wriggling to get free.

While we had been binding them, I had explained my very loose theory to Frank. My hypothesis was that if a hypnotist could induce a state where they acted as zombies and would continue to do so until they were given a code word, or in the case of the zombie granny, given such a shock that they were brought back from their reverie, then that was what we were witnessing. I further hypothesised that the drug found in Edna's blood was going to be the tetrodotoxin stuff that James had been talking about earlier or some derivative thereof. This was either how he got them into the state to induce such a deep hypnosis or how he kept them there. I was stretching, I knew it. However, it was the only idea I had. The only question that remained was *why*?

With our two zombies immobile and the crowd of people in the previously busy street now thinning, I hooked the backpack over my shoulder and set off down the road toward The Casino Nightclub where I hoped to find some answers. I did not ask Frank to come along, I had no wish to place him or anyone else in danger, but I expected he would follow me anyway. He did.

'Is there a plan?' He asked as we began to meet with smoke. I could not see the origin of it but remembered the news report saying that fires had been started at the previous zombie attack sites.

'The plan is...' I started to explain but I failed to finish as a zombie crashed through a store front window to my right and grabbed me. The zombie was a strong, athletic, twenty-something guy who was taller and heavier than me and had caught me by surprise. I went down underneath him, toppled by his momentum, my right arm and the zombie twatting stick it held pinned beneath me and my left arm in his grip. He bit into my shoulder. Even with three layers on it still hurt and I started to see the benefit of the zombie armour Frank had placed in the back pack.

I flipped and shoved him away and managed to slide my arm out from underneath me. Athlete zombie's teeth lost their purchase as I did, however he just lunged for my face and would have bitten a chunk right out of me had I not shoved the end of the twatting stick directly into his open mouth. Frank grabbed his shoulders in a bid to wrestle him away from me and between us we managed to get me out from beneath the man. I was still trying to avoid hurting him, convinced as I was that he was just some bloke that had been drugged and hypnotised.

'Grab the duct tape!' I yelled to Frank.

'We might need a plan B.' Frank said, lifting the pack and backing away.

I turned to see what he was looking at. Six more zombies coming right at us, shuffling and groaning and looking hungry.

Bugger.

My intention to avoid hurting anyone was looking doubtful. Accepting it, I rolled away from athlete zombie and kicked him hard in the side of the head as I went. Noble concept abandoned, my new plan was to survive.

'Frank, find a weapon. This is about to get real.' I shouted to psyche myself up.

I lifted the zombie twatting stick, ready to use it as Frank appeared beside me with a katana. 'Dammit Frank, No.' I screeched. 'These are fake, hypnotised zombies. You can't kill them. Injuries will be hard enough to explain to them when they come around. Put the sheath on it and bash them with it. Okay?'

'Yes. Yes, of course.' He mumbled, somewhat embarrassed by his own bravado. Then they were upon us. With weapons to hit them, they were easy enough to put down but there were more coming. The smoke swirled, shrouding us like a thick cloak, caught between the buildings on a breezeless day. In the last five minutes we had barely progressed down the road towards the Casino Nightclub and the lack of advancement was beginning to annoy me.

'We need to get to the nightclub, Frank. They don't move fast, so we are going to charge through them. Right?'

'Okay.' He replied, clearly nervous and trying hard to ignore it.

Not bothering to offer any further explanation, I steeled myself to charge through the line of zombies that came at us. I grabbed the shoulder of Frank's jacket, so I would not lose him, then broke into a sprint.

Then stopped.

Stumbling towards me from the smoke was James. There were maybe another ten zombies around him, some ahead, some behind but all coming towards us as we were the only people remaining in the street. Everyone else had fled. He was stumbling along in the group, arms out and groaning like the rest. Where the zombies' eyes were deranged though, his were just terrified. He spotted me and risked a wry smile.

He was faking!

The zombies were upon us again, so I hit the first one over the head as gently as one can with a wooden club, then ducked into the lunge of the next one and whacked him under the chin.

'James!' I yelled. 'Crouch down.'

He looked confused but obeyed the instruction. I still had one hand on Frank's jacket in fear of being split up. 'OK, Frank. Let's go!' I found myself yelling again. What can I say? It was an exciting situation.

At a charge, we closed the distance to James, knocking zombies over like pins as we went. It proved to be much, much easier than trying to knock them out without hurting them. Frank and I scooped an arm each without even slowing down and we were running down the road with James between us, his heels dragging along the concrete

More smoke swirled around us and I spotted fire behind a window as flames were licking at the woodwork inside. Sirens could be heard in the distance; police and fire brigade and probably paramedics. All were needed.

Suddenly, the smoke cleared, we were just metres from the Casino Nightclub entrance and there were no zombies in sight. I dragged James and Frank through the open door of the Victoria and Eagle pub to get us off the street. Checking that nobody, and no zombies were inside, I slammed the door behind us. It felt slightly safer for a moment.

'What is going on?' James asked between deep breaths.

Now that we had at least a few seconds to re-group I had questions for him. 'James did the hypnotist create the zombies?'

'Yeah! He did!' He replied, astounded. 'How did you know?'

'Lucky guess.' I said rather than waste time on conversation. 'Next question. How are you not affected?'

'Oh. Well, when we arrived, the chap had an assistant lady and she was handing out canapes. She was very insistent that everyone have one, but it smelled like fish and since I am a vegan, I faked putting it in my mouth and slipped it into my pocket instead. Here it is.' He announced producing a rather fancy, but now sadly battered blini looking object, with a leaf, a blob of something edible and a shake of spice over the top.

'Thank you.' I said, taking the canape and placing it into a little bag I had pulled from one of my many pockets. An investigator keeps things like that just in case evidence pops up. 'Then what?'

'The Great Howsini asked everyone to sit and launched into his show. It was weird though, not like his usual act and I noticed that everyone around me had stopped moving. It was like they were unconscious, but their eyes were still wide open. The weirdest thing was that he was telling them all that they were the walking dead, the most terrifying zombie creatures that needed to feed on human flesh. I was scared because they were all starting to groan and make growling noises, so I played along. The assistant lady threw open the doors and he sent us all out to *kill, kill, kill.* That was what he said, "*Kill, kill, kill!*"

Right then. 'Gents you can come with me if you want, but you may be safer staying here. The Great Howsini is about to learn the error of his ways.' I was going to find this idiot and punch him in the pants. Bring zombies to my town, real or not and you pay for it. The problem being, that I had no idea how to find him.

'James do you have a picture of him, or can you describe him?' I was hoping he was going to be easy to spot and that I could catch him here. If not, I would catch up to him later, but by then the adrenalin would be out of my system, I would be thinking with more reason and would find it far harder to justify hurting him.

'No need really.' James said. 'That's him over there.' He pointed.

Across the street, a man in a suit that screamed *stage show act* with its sequinned seam up the trouser leg and overly long jacket tails, was carrying heavy sacks towards the car park. He was in his late thirties, a good fifty pounds overweight and had very little hair left. What there was formed a black ring around the sides and back of his scalp. The effect making his scalp look like a round mountain rising above particularly dark clouds. Behind him, a woman of similar age and figure was weighed down by more sacks. I pulled out my camera and started filming. Then, I handed it to James with the simple instruction to keep it rolling.

The Great Howsini's real name was Dave Gough. The lady was his wife, Brenda. She was a chemist. Once cornered, they had given in immediately and confessed their story to the police that had arrived on the scene moments later. I was getting to be known by the local police as my job had a habit of landing me in the vicinity of dubious events. But for once, they had skipped over the bit where they arrested me and had allowed me to remain at the scene. The Goughs were caught red-handed with bags of cash and goods stolen from shops, bars and restaurants that they had subsequently set ablaze in order to cover their tracks. Missing money and goods would be discovered at the other zombie attack sites when the ash was sifted.

James's original research into how to make a zombie had been bang on the money. Brenda was a chemist by trade and could legally obtain the tetrodotoxin which she had made it into a drug that would render a person ingesting it in a state of semi-suspended animation. Full of ego, she had bragged how deliciously complex it had been.

The police had departed with the Goughs in cuffs and we trudged wearily back through a desolated and partly destroyed Rochester High Street. We passed fire brigade teams putting out fires and we paused at my office to lock up, and at Frank's bookshop, where we found the door wide open, but the contents unmolested.

I was bitten, battered, bruised and tired, but also somehow elated. It was time for a cold one and I was buying.

The End

Except it still isn't. Check the next page!

Note from the Author:

Hi there,

That's the end of the short story collection for now, I'm afraid. Each of those stories is part of wider series which you can explore by clicking the links on the next few pages.

My love for writing started at school in the seventies when creating my own characters and stories was about the only class I enjoyed. Life as an author wasn't something my parents could perceive as a career and I was terrible at everything else, so unquestioningly, I followed family tradition and joined the armed forces.

I cannot say the twenty-five years spent in the British Army was a waste of my time, but I certainly wish I had chosen to pursue a career as a writer a lot earlier. I could have combined the two, but always found other things that I needed to do instead of sitting down to craft my magnum opus.

So it was in my forties that I finally published my first book and I really haven't looked back. I was able to quit the terrible soul-sucking corporate job and go full time just two years after publishing that first book and now my life is about filling your bookshelf with wonderfully suspense-filled yet funny mystery and adventure books. I seem to have found my niche, or perhaps I should call it my brand. There is no profanity in my books, I have never found it necessary, and there is never any graphic descriptions of sex or violence.

The fight scenes – there has to be some – are told with a degree of experience as I not only spent years practicing various martial arts, the Army insisted I also learn to box, and then there were semi-regular events where enemy combatants would try to kill me with guns, bombs, mortar rounds and various other deadly devices.

Despite my background, or perhaps because of it, I write tales that would be shown on PBS or Hallmark channel on a Sunday afternoon. They are cozy, and told with tenderness and emotion because I am kind of guy who cannot watch *Steel Magnolias* without blubbing.

I think that's enough about me. If you want to know more there is a regular newsletter you can sign up below. I give away audiobooks and hold competitions for people to get their names into the dedication section of the books. Plus you get cover reveals, leaked first chapters, insights into what is coming and much, much more. Or you can just buy the books. You choice entirely.

Take care

Steve Higgs

Read the book that started it all.

A thirty-year-old priceless jewel theft and a man who really has been stabbed in the back. Can a 52-year-old, slightly plump housewife unravel the mystery in time to save herself from jail?

When housewife, Patricia, catches her husband in bed with her best friend, her reaction isn't to rant and yell. Instead, she calmly empties the bank accounts and boards the first cruise ship she sees in nearby Southampton.

There she meets the unfairly handsome captain and her appointed butler for the trip – that's what you get when the only room available is a royal suite! But with most of the money gone and sleeping off a gin-fuelled pity party for one, she wakes to find herself accused of murder; she was seen leaving the bar with the victim and her purse is in his cabin.

Certain that all she did last night was fall into bed, a race against time begins as she tries to work out what happened and clear her name. But the Deputy Captain, the man responsible for safety and security onboard, has confined her to her cabin and has no interest in her version of events. Worse yet, as she begins to dig into the dead man's past, she uncovers a secret - there's a giant stolen sapphire somewhere and people are prepared to kill to get their hands on it.

With only a Jamaican butler faking an English accent and a pretty gym instructor to help, she must piece together the clues and do it fast. Or when she gets off the ship in St Kitts, she'll be in cuffs!

Pork Pie Pandemonium

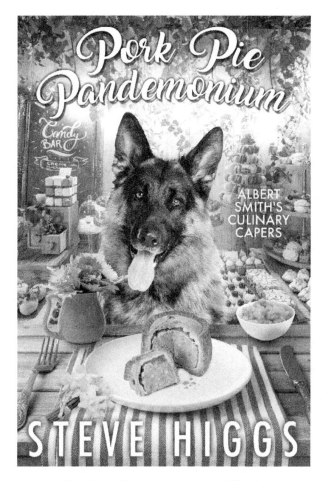

Baking. It can get a guy killed.

When a retired detective superintendent chooses to take a culinary tour of the British Isles, he hopes to find tasty treats and delicious bakes …

… what he finds is a clue to a crime in the ingredients for his pork pie.

His dog, Rex Harrison, an ex-police dog fired for having a bad attitude, cannot understand why the humans are struggling to solve the mystery. He can already smell the answer – it's right before their noses.

He'll pitch in to help his human and the shop owner's teenage daughter as the trio set out to save the shop from closure. Is the rival pork pie shop across the street to blame? Or is there something far more sinister going on?

One thing is for sure, what started out as a bit of fun, is getting deadlier by the hour, and they'd better work out what the dog knows soon or it could be curtains for them all.

Under a Blue Moon

Tempest Michaels is about to have a bad week.

When a newspaper ad typo sends all manner of daft paranormal enquiries his way, P.I. Tempest Michaels has no sense of the trouble and danger heading his way.

In no time at all, he has multiple cases to investigate, but it's all ridiculous nonsense like minor celebrity Richard Claythorn, who believes he is being stalked by a werewolf and a shopkeeper in a nearby village with an invisible thief.

Solving these cases might be fun if his demanding mother (Why are there no grandchildren, Tempest?) didn't insist on going with him, but the simple case of celebrity stalking might not be all it seems when he catches a man lurking behind the client's property just in time to see him step into the moonlight and begin to transform.

All he wanted was a nice easy job where he got to be his own boss and could take his trusty Dachshunds to work. How much trouble can a typo cause?

The paranormal? It's all nonsense, but proving it might get him killed.

Untethered Magic

STEVE HIGGS
THE REALM OF FALSE GODS

UNTETHERED MAGIC
A WIZARD IN BREMEN
PART ONE

Today's tasks:
1. Escape from underground cell
2. Recruit snarky d-bag werewolf to help
3. Invade demon realm and rescue a girl

For wizard detective, Otto Schneider, magic has always kept him out of trouble. Now it's working in reverse …

… and he's just started the fight of his life.

There's an ancient secret buried in the Earth's past and he just uncovered it. Magical beings once ruled over us until their betrayed leader made a death curse with his final breath. Banished from the realm of man for over four thousand years, the curse is weakening, and these beings, these … demons, are coming back to rule the Earth once more.

They are powerful, immortal and unstoppable, but they don't know everything. They left some of their magic behind and their return has sparked an awakening.

Heroes will rise …

More Books by Steve Higgs

Blue Moon Investigations

Patricia Fisher Cruise Mysteries

Patricia Fisher Mystery Adventures

What Sam Knew

Solstice Goat

Recipe for Murder

A Banshee and a Bookshop

Diamonds, Dinner Jackets, and Death

Frozen Vengeance

Mug Shot

Albert Smith Culinary Capers

Pork Pie Pandemonium

Bakewell Tart Bludgeoning

Stilton Slaughter

Bedfordshire Clanger Calamity

Death of a Yorkshire Pudding

The Realm of False Gods

Untethered magic

Unleashed Magic

Early Shift

Damaged but Powerful

Demon Bound

Familiar Territory

The Armour of God

Free Books and More

Get sneak peaks, exclusive giveaways, behind the scenes content, and more. Plus, you'll be notified of Fan Pricing events when they occur and get exclusive offers from other authors because all UF writers are automatically friends.

Not only that, but you'll receive an exclusive FREE story staring Otto and Zachary and two free stories from the author's Blue Moon Investigations series.

Yes, please! Sign me up for lots of FREE stuff and bargains!

Want to follow me and keep up with what I am doing?

Facebook

Printed in Great Britain
by Amazon

40458781R00099